I0793773

SECRETS of the DEAD

For Tegen.
Because brilliant editors never get the credit they deserve.
M. R.

For the Duck Duck Moose group.
G. W.

With special thanks to Dr. Daniel Antoine at
the British Museum for his contribution and advice.

First published 2022 by Nosy Crow Ltd.
Wheat Wharf, 27a Shad Thames
London, SE1 2XZ, UK

This edition published 2025 by Nosy Crow Inc.
145 Lincoln Road
Lincoln, MA 01773, USA

www.nosycrow.us

ISBN 979-8-88777-081-9

Library of Congress Catalog Card Number pending.

Printed in Shenzhen, China, following rigorous ethical sourcing standards.

1 3 5 7 9 10 8 6 4 2

The British Museum

nosy crow

written by
Matt Ralphs

illustrated by
Gordy Wright

SECRETS of the DEAD

Mummies and Other Human Remains from Around the World

Contents

Europe and the Middle East

Asia

Introducing the Dead

The remains of our ancestors are all around us. They lie in graveyards, cemeteries, churches, and temples, stone tombs and burial mounds. Most cultures throughout history believed it was important to treat the dead with care, and many approaches have been used to either lay to rest, preserve, or respectfully dispose of human remains.

Sometimes bones are even turned into works of art and put on display. In St. Michael's Chapel in Hallstatt, Austria, hundreds of beautifully painted skulls are stored, some decorated with wreaths, flowers, colored crosses, and the dead person's name and year of their death. Tunnels under Paris that were once ancient stone quarries now house the remains of millions of people—their skulls and bones lining walls in ordered layers. The ancient skeleton of a man named Saint Pancratius was even given a spectacular suit of armor.

Painted Skulls
St. Michael's Chapel, Austria

Egyptian scarab amulet
(found by M. Ralphs)

Saint Pancratius
Church of St. Nikolaus, Switzerland

In most environments, when someone dies their body's soft tissues decay over time, leaving only the skeleton—skull, bones, and teeth—behind. However, in mummified remains, soft tissues are preserved; they come to us in a more complete form. When we look at a mummy, we are reminded of the person they used to be and can learn about the time and place they lived in, from the food that they ate to the diseases they suffered from.

The Archaeologist's Handbook

Beauty of Xiaohe
Taklamakan Desert, China

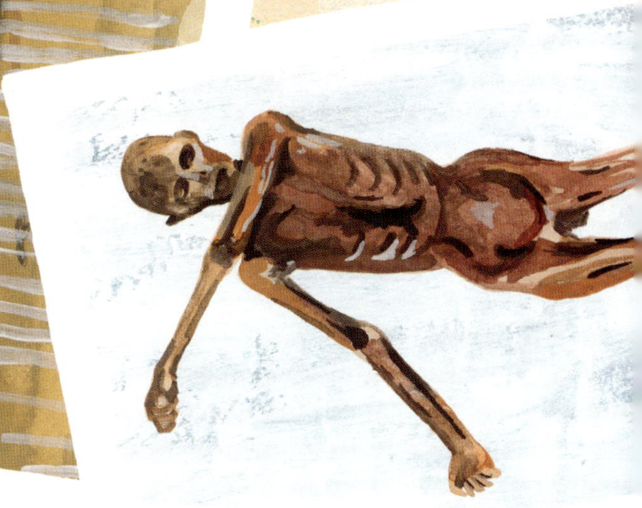

Ötzi the Ice Man
Ötzal Alps, Italy

Some mummies were naturally created by chance. A man we now call Ötzi died high up in the alps of northern Italy that border Austria; he was covered in ice for 5,000 years, which acted just like a freezer, preserving even the tattoos on his skin. Others were deliberately mummified to stop their bodies from decaying. The ancient Egyptians are the most famous, but other cultures prepared their dead to ensure preservation—like the mysterious Chinchorro of South America, or the Scythians of Siberia.

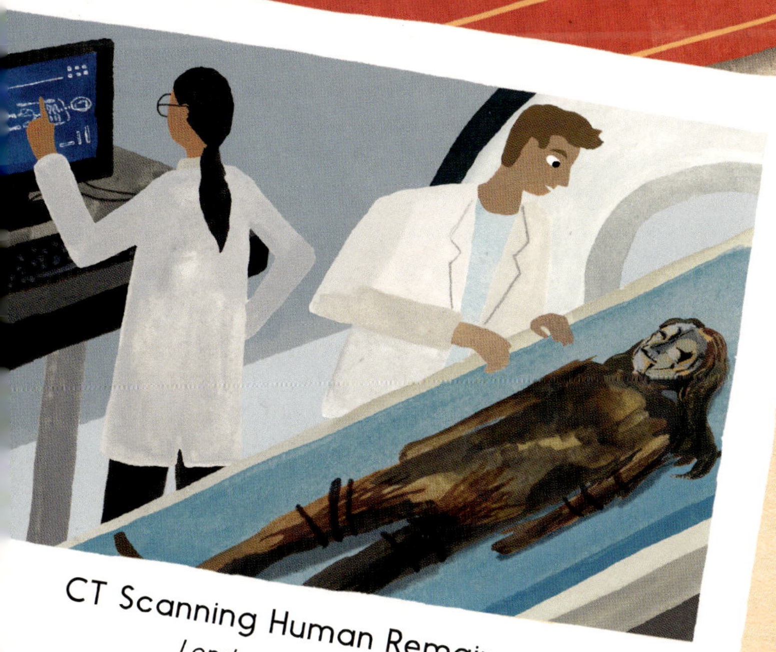

CT Scanning Human Remains
London, England

The mummified dead have fascinated the living for centuries. Wealthy Victorians even held "unwrapping parties," where people gathered to watch Egyptian mummies being stripped of their linen bandages. Nowadays, the dead are treated with more respect, and when archaeologists examine the delicate human remains in their care, they use modern technology like X-rays and CT scans to avoid any unnecessary damage.

This book will show you the amazing discoveries researchers have made and reveal the many secrets of the dead.

Tutankhamun

In November 1922, British archaeologist Howard Carter peered through a hole in the sealed doorway of a tomb. As his eyes adjusted to the dark chamber beyond, he saw a vast collection of extraordinary and beautiful objects. Carter's companion asked, "Can you see anything?" Carter replied, "Yes, wonderful things!"

Carter had discovered the tomb of Tutankhamun who, in 1333 BC, became King of Egypt at the age of about nine. He died only ten years later. In paintings from his tomb he hunts wild animals and fights battles in his chariot; his stunning golden funerary mask shows a handsome, noble face. But art is not always true to life, so we need to examine his mummy to discover who he really was.

Tutankhamun's fragile remains were damaged during examination in the 1920s. Nowadays, by using computers and X-ray machines, scientists have learned far more about the boy king without even touching him. Their studies revealed a very different person to the energetic warrior king shown in the paintings. Tutankhamun was slender, with narrow shoulders and wide hips.

Tutankhamun appears to have suffered from a bone disease that deformed his toes and caused his left foot to twist inward. Walking may have been extremely painful, and it's likely he used a stick to help him get around. Some experts think that he also had malaria, a disease spread by mosquito bites that causes periods of nausea, headaches, and fever.

Scans show that at some point Tutankhamun fractured his left thigh, perhaps during a fall. We cannot be sure, but it's possible Tutankhamun's early death was caused by the malaria, the fracture, an infection, or a combination of all these factors.

Many objects inside the tomb were decorated with the "Wedjat," or the "Eye of Horus," which was a symbol of protection and good health.

130 sticks were found in the tomb. Some were for walking, and others for killing snakes.

Several beautiful "pectorals" were found in the tomb. They were large pieces of jewelry worn on the chest.

An iron dagger with an ornamental golden sheath was discovered and is thought to be made from a fallen meteorite.

A pair of sandals were found with portraits of Tutankhamun's enemies on the soles.

Known throughout the world, Tutankhamun is more famous today than he was when he was alive. People travel from all over the world to gaze at the fragile and fascinating remains of a young man who, 3,300 years ago, was the ruler of one of the most powerful civilizations on the planet.

Ramses the Great

Ramses II was worshipped like a god during his 66-year reign (1279–1213 BC). He won many battles and erected magnificent temples, monuments, and statues. Under his rule, Egypt grew to the height of its power.

But even godlike kings die, and when Ramses passed away at around the age of 90 he was buried in the Valley of the Kings, where tombs were built into cliffs. He was later moved several times until eventually ending up in a secret tomb where he lay undisturbed until local villagers discovered him by chance in the late 1800s.

Ramses' preserved body gives us clues as to what he was like in life. He was 5.6 feet tall, with a sharp-featured face, strong jaw, and aquiline nose. The back and sides of his head are still covered in thick, wavy hair; sparse tufts cling to his temples and mostly bald scalp. His once white hair is now reddish in color, perhaps stained during the mummification process.

Ramses may have been a great king, but scientific studies of his mummy showed he still suffered from ordinary illnesses. He was probably debilitated by arthritis, a painful disease that caused his joints to swell and made him walk with a stoop. Over the years, fat built up on the inside of his arteries, making them narrower. This caused poor blood circulation and increased his risk of heart disease. Scientists also found that he had a painful dental abscess; these occur when pus builds up inside the jawbone due to an infection in the teeth.

Even after 3,200 years, Ramses still looks every inch a king. His head, with its chiseled features, is stern and dignified. His linen-wrapped hands are especially well-preserved, and the way he holds them away from his chest makes it look as if this great pharaoh is waking up and beginning to move.

Ramses was buried in the Valley of the Kings in a tomb we now call KV7. It's located opposite the tomb of his many sons, which is the largest in the valley with at least 130 chambers. The walls are decorated with many scenes, including the Opening of the Mouth ceremony (page 17), and Ramses himself. The only objects found inside were a wooden shabti figurine, pieces of glass, jar lids, and statue fragments. Unfortunately, Ramses' resting place has been damaged over the years by floods.

Gebelein Man

One of the earliest Egyptians whose body survives died 5,500 years ago at the age of about 19, many years before the rule of the pharaohs began in around 3000 BC. Excavated by archaeologists in the late 19th century, he was given the name Gebelein Man because he was found near the town of Gebelein. We will never know his real name, but we can discover other facts about him by examining his incredibly well-preserved remains.

Gebelein Man was buried inside a shallow grave in the desert. His people laid him on his side facing west. He has a full set of healthy teeth and tufts of red hair on his scalp. His legs are drawn up to his chest, and one hand covers his face as if trying to block out the light.

The shape of his bones can be clearly seen through skin that is blotched and the color of ancient parchment. CT scans revealed that his skull still contains the dried remains of his brain.

What looks like a smudge on his upper arm is actually one of the oldest tattoos in the world, showing a bull and a Barbary sheep.

Gebelein Man's remarkable preservation occurred naturally. The hot desert sand and dry conditions dried out his body, preventing it from rotting away to just a skeleton. Some archaeologists believe that when later ancient Egyptians found naturally created mummies like Gebelein Man, it gave them the idea to deliberately preserve their dead.

In the British Museum, Gebelein Man is shown surrounded by the types of items that were sometimes buried alongside bodies during this period: clay pots and jars decorated with patterns and images, and jewelry made from beads.

In 2012, scientists created an incredibly detailed 3D image of Gebelein Man using an X-ray machine called a CT scanner. This revealed the dark truth of how this young man met his end. A puncture wound under his left shoulder blade proves that he was killed by someone wielding a copper or flint knife. The force of the blow was so strong it shattered a rib and punctured the lung beneath. Because Gebelein Man was stabbed in the back, he probably never even saw the blow coming. The murderer's identity and motive are secrets we'll never know.

Preserving the Dead

During their 3,000-year-long civilization, the ancient Egyptians perfected the art of preserving their dead. Not only does each mummy provide us with priceless historical information from the distant past, but when we look at their faces we also see fellow human beings who spoke, smiled, and lived just as we do.

Fit for a King

The most effective mummification method was only used on pharaohs, their families, and wealthy individuals who could afford it. It was messy, difficult, and took a lot of time and skill to complete. The idea was to stop the body from rotting away by removing the water and some of the internal organs. This tricky job was done by special embalmers (embalm is another word for mummify).

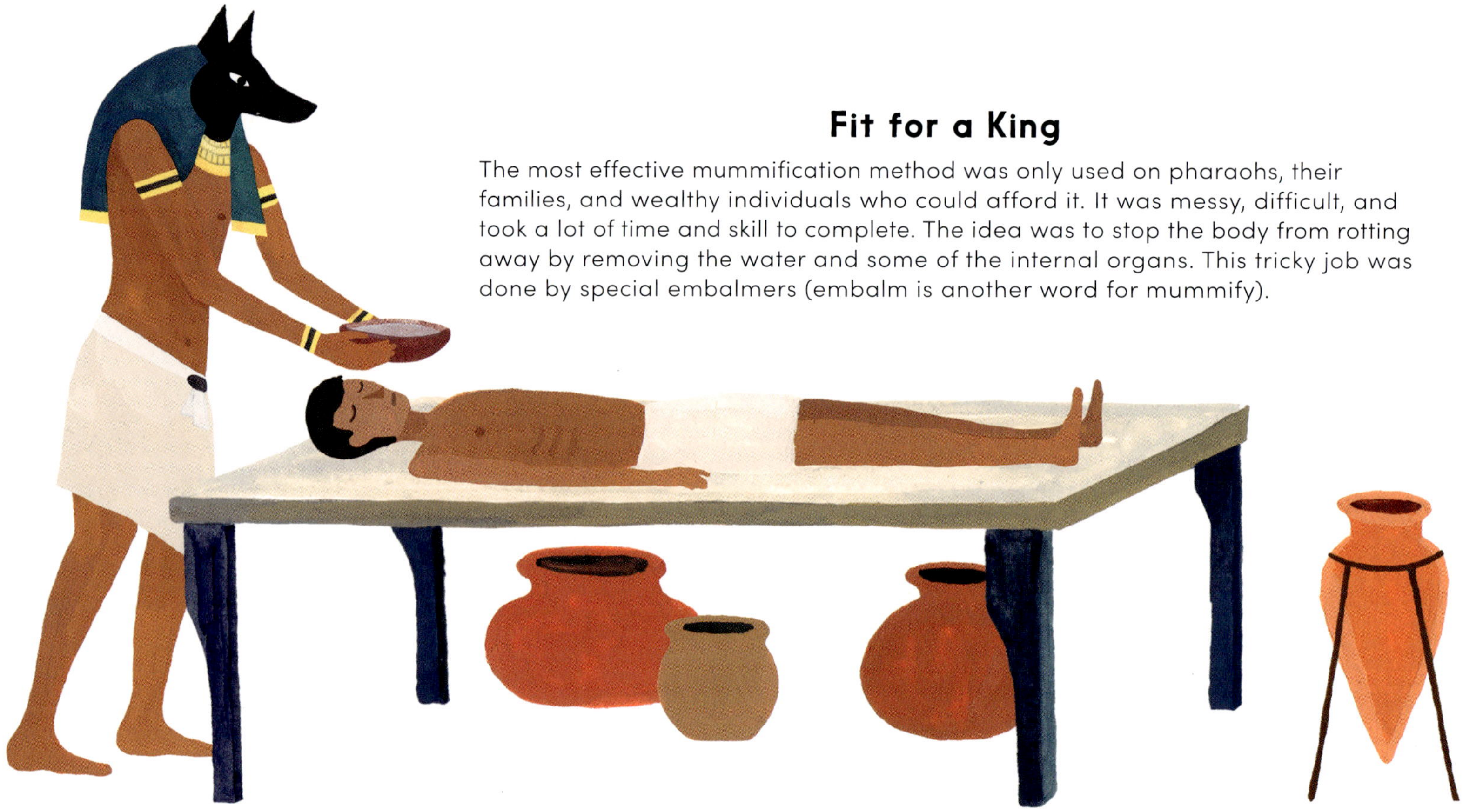

Brain Removal

After washing the corpse, one of the first things the embalmers did was remove the brain. They inserted a long rod with a hook on the end up the person's nostril and deep inside the skull. The brain was then carefully drawn out with the hook, and any remaining liquid was allowed to drain from the nose.

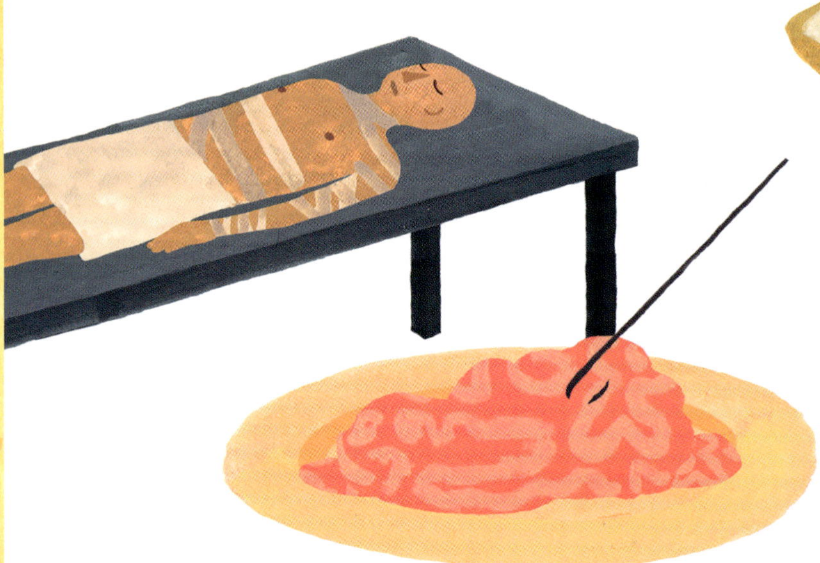

Organ Removal

The embalmer then made a cut in the person's side and pulled out their lungs, liver, stomach, and intestines (see page 16). The organs were slippery, and any incense used by the embalmers would not have completely disguised the smell. The heart, which the ancient Egyptians believed contained a person's soul, memories, and intelligence, was left inside the chest—the person would need it in the afterlife.

Drying the Flesh

After being washed with scented oils, the inside of the body was packed with bags of natron—a type of natural salt—to dry out the soft tissues. The embalmers then covered the body with more natron, which drew out all the moisture and prevented it from rotting away.

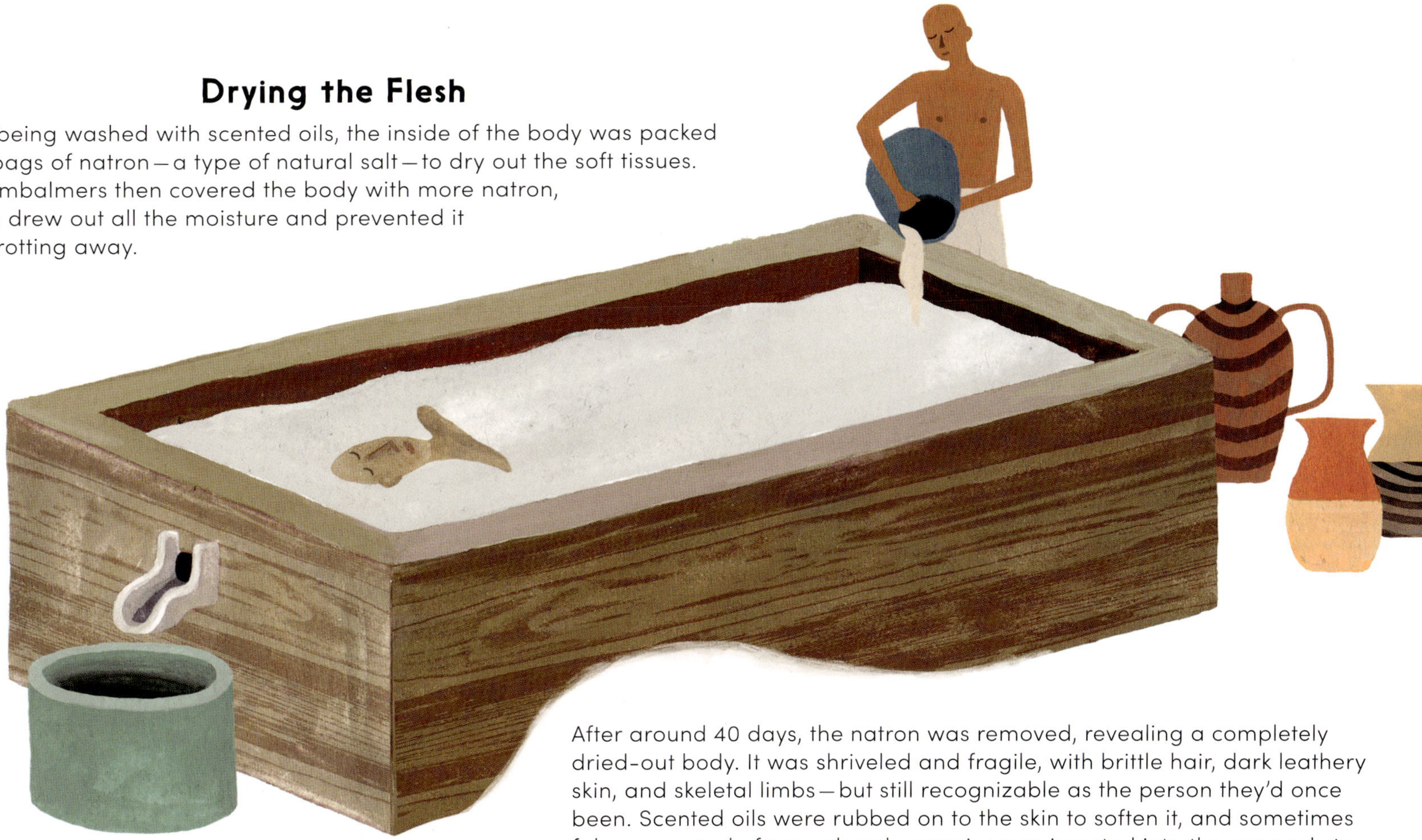

After around 40 days, the natron was removed, revealing a completely dried-out body. It was shriveled and fragile, with brittle hair, dark leathery skin, and skeletal limbs—but still recognizable as the person they'd once been. Scented oils were rubbed on to the skin to soften it, and sometimes false eyes made from colored ceramic were inserted into the eye sockets.

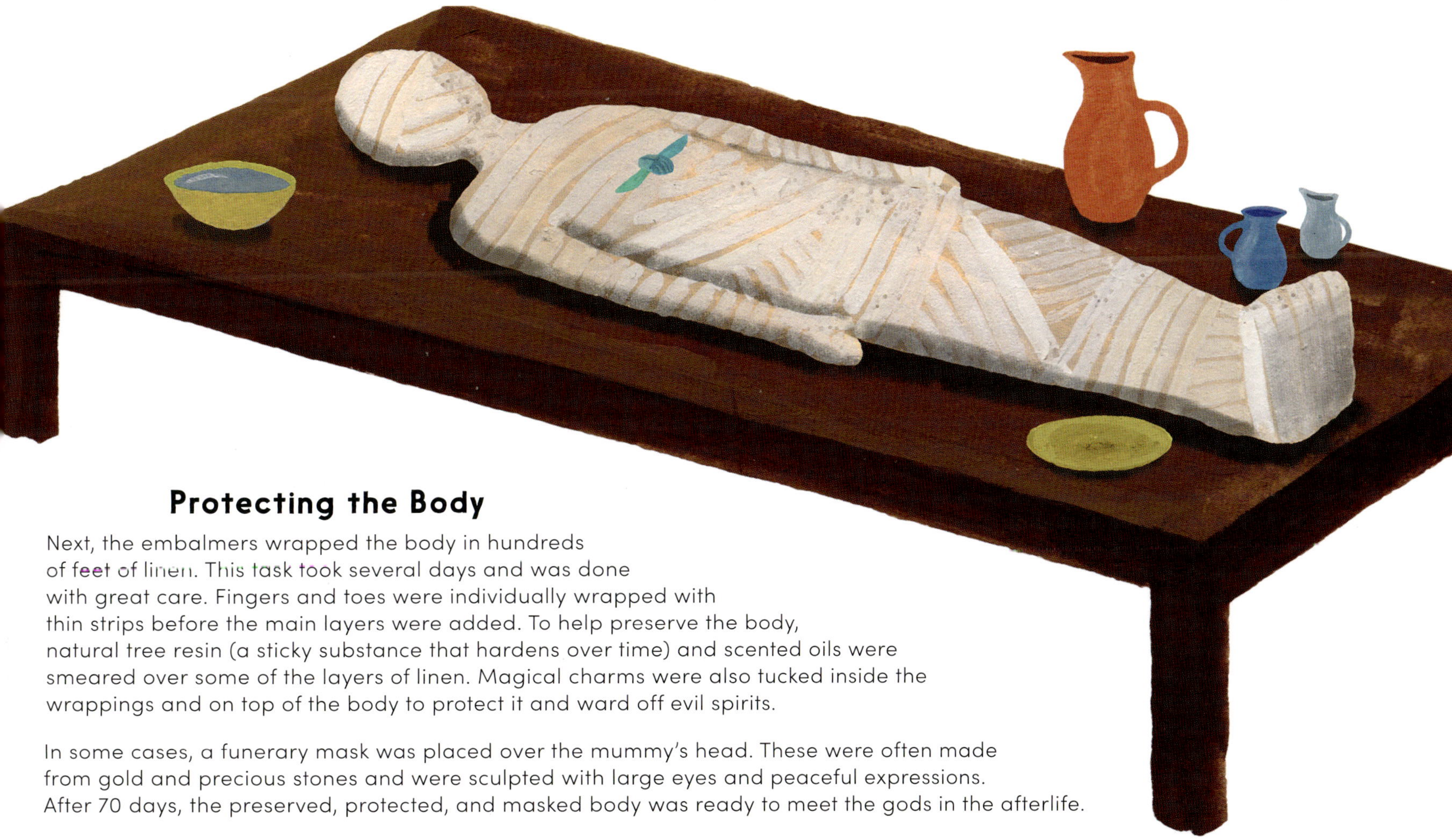

Protecting the Body

Next, the embalmers wrapped the body in hundreds of feet of linen. This task took several days and was done with great care. Fingers and toes were individually wrapped with thin strips before the main layers were added. To help preserve the body, natural tree resin (a sticky substance that hardens over time) and scented oils were smeared over some of the layers of linen. Magical charms were also tucked inside the wrappings and on top of the body to protect it and ward off evil spirits.

In some cases, a funerary mask was placed over the mummy's head. These were often made from gold and precious stones and were sculpted with large eyes and peaceful expressions. After 70 days, the preserved, protected, and masked body was ready to meet the gods in the afterlife.

Canopic Jars

The ancient Egyptians believed that to reach the afterlife, a dead person's soul needed a preserved body (the mummy) and intact internal organs. After taking out the organs, the embalmers dried them with natron and wrapped them up in strips of linen. Safe from decay, the organs were put on top of or replaced inside the body.

They could also be stored separately inside stone or pottery containers called canopic jars. Canopic jar lids were often made to look like the heads of four protective gods:

Human-headed Imsety guarded the liver.

Baboon-headed Hapi guarded the lungs.

Falcon-headed Qebehsenuef guarded the intestines.

Jackal-headed Duamutef guarded the stomach.

Animal Mummies

Ancient Egyptians mummified animals, too. Certain species—like baboons and crocodiles—were closely associated with the gods, and thousands (or in the case of cats, millions) were mummified and left as offerings at temples. The animal bodies were dried out, filled with sand and earth, and wrapped in linen.

Life, Death, Afterlife

The ancient Egyptians built many enormous stone pyramids and tombs chiseled into rock for their dead. These monuments were expensive, needed thousands of workers, and often took decades to complete. Why did the ancient Egyptians spend so much time and energy on buildings meant only for the dead? The answer lies in their beliefs in life, death, and the afterlife.

The ancient Egyptians believed that death was not the end of a person's existence, but a doorway to reach a wonderful new home. Imagine golden wheat fields swaying in the breeze, a wide blue river reflecting a wide blue sky, the sun on your back, and the taste of honey on your lips. This afterlife of everlasting happiness (one of many that the ancient Egyptians believed in throughout their history) was called the Field of Reeds and everyone, from farmer to pharaoh, wanted to get there.

An ancient Egyptian knew exactly what was required to reach the Field of Reeds after their death. First, the dead person needed their body to be mummified so it could serve as an eternal home for their spirit.

Next, the person's soul—which left the body at the point of death—had to be encouraged to return. This was done at the funeral during a ceremony called the Opening of the Mouth. By touching the mummy's eyes, ears, nose, and mouth with a special axe-like tool called an "adze," the priest reawoke the deceased's senses and invited the soul to re-enter the body. With body and soul reunited and its senses alert, the mummy was considered alive.

The deceased then had to find their way from the tomb, through a dangerous shadowland filled with demons, traps, and fiery lakes, to a place called the Hall of Two Truths. There they met Osiris, god of the Underworld, and faced the Weighing of the Heart ceremony.

The person's heart was placed on a set of scales. If it was heavy with sin, the scales would tip and the person would suffer a "second death." But if they had led a good life, the scales would balance and Osiris would allow them entrance into the Field of Reeds to live in perfect happiness forever.

Ancient Egyptian Funerary Gods

Anubis: Jackal-headed god of death, mummification, and the Underworld.

Osiris: Human-headed god of fertility, resurrection, and life.

Thoth: Ibis-headed god of writing who recorded the results of the Weighing of the Heart.

Ammut: Crocodile-headed goddess who devoured the hearts of the unworthy dead.

Houses of the Dead

The types of building that pharaohs were buried in changed over the millennia. Whatever the design, they needed to be dry, strong, and secure enough to keep the body and the treasures alongside it preserved and undisturbed for eternity.

Mastaba Tombs

The earliest pharaohs were buried in mastaba tombs. These were large, mud-brick buildings with sloping walls and a flat roof. The body was laid to rest in a chamber cut deep into the ground, safe from scavenging animals. Impressive as they were, mastaba tombs were nowhere near as remarkable as what the ancient Egyptians came up with next.

The Step Pyramid

A pharaoh named Djoser (who reigned 2630–2611 BC) did not want to be buried in a traditional mastaba tomb so he ordered his chief architect, Imhotep, to design something spectacular. Imhotep did as he was asked and, by adding five more limestone layers—each one smaller than the last—to an existing mastaba tomb, he created the first ever pyramid. His step pyramid was so successful that it still stands today, 4,700 years later.

Secret Tombs

Many pharaohs built their own spectacular pyramids, but these were easy targets for thieves, and most were soon robbed of their treasures. So, from the 16th century BC, pharaohs tried to keep their valuables safe by building secret tombs into the cliffs of the Valley of the Kings.

Stairways, passages, treasure rooms, and burial chambers were chiseled into solid rock, plastered smooth, and then intricately painted with hieroglyphs (the ancient Egyptians' writing system) and images of the gods.

The Great Pyramid

Imhotep's revolutionary step pyramid design started the trend for pyramid building. A later pharaoh named Sneferu (who reigned 2575–2551 BC) introduced pyramids with smooth, sloping sides of polished limestone. Many more like this followed, the largest and most spectacular being Pharaoh Khufu's Great Pyramid at Giza, the only surviving Ancient Wonder of the World.

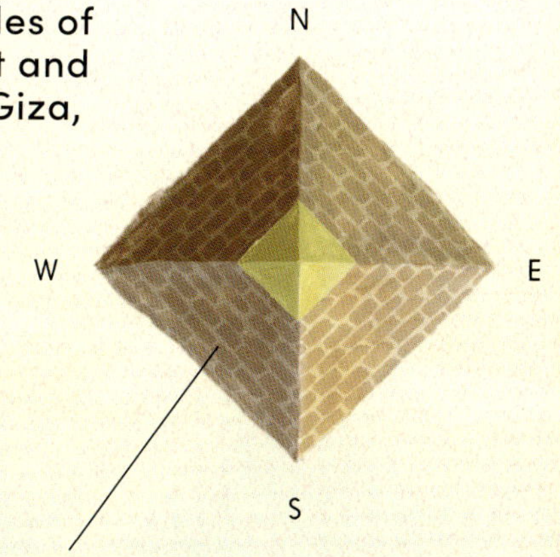

The Great Pyramid was built by thousands of skilled workers for Pharaoh Khufu, who came to the throne in 2551 BC. At both its original height (481.4 feet) and its current height (449 feet), the Great Pyramid is taller than the Taj Mahal (240 feet), the Statue of Liberty (305 feet), and the London Eye (443 feet). It was the tallest structure in the world for 3,800 years until Lincoln Cathedral topped it at 525 feet in 1311 AD. Each side is exactly 755 feet long at the base and corresponds precisely to the four points of the compass.

The pyramid's approximately 2.3 million limestone blocks weighed an average of 2.5 tons each. Many experts believe that after being quarried and shaped, the blocks were hauled up ramps by groups of men and maneuvered into place using rollers and levers. This task required superhuman amounts of effort; some of the granite blocks in the King's Chamber weigh an incredible 80 tons (about the same as twelve elephants). They were quarried 500 miles away and transported by boat to the building site.

Each side was faced with polished white limestone, and the peak capped with a gold and silver combination called "electrum." This luminous building, called "the Horizon of Khufu" by the ancient Egyptians, must have dazzled the people who gazed at it.

Inside the pyramid are three rooms—the Lower, Queen's, and King's Chambers—connected by long, sloping passages. The Lower Chamber is cut deep into the rock beneath the pyramid's base, and its purpose is a mystery. The Queen's Chamber has a small hole in the wall that might have contained a statue. The King's Chamber contains Khufu's lidless sarcophagus (stone coffin).

The massive stone blocks sealing the entrance did not stop tomb robbers from getting inside and stripping the pyramid bare of treasures—including Khufu himself.

The Maiden of Llullaillaco

In 1999, at the top of a mountain in northwest Argentina, South America, archaeologists discovered the near-perfectly preserved body of a young Inca girl. Sitting slightly slumped, with closed eyes, a peaceful expression, and hands resting in her lap, she looked as if she was asleep. What circumstances, 500 years ago, led to her death in such a cold and lonely spot?

The Inca created an empire in South America's steaming jungles and snow-capped mountains that lasted from 1438 to 1533 AD. Approximately 12 million people were ruled by an all-powerful emperor, called the Sapa Inca. Impressive builders, they constructed monumental stone fortresses like Machu Picchu and an enormous road network that crossed some of the most difficult ground in the world—and all without the aid of iron tools or the wheel. Most ordinary Inca lived in villages. They grew maize and potatoes, tended alpacas, enjoyed family gatherings, brewed beer, played music, and wove beautifully patterned textiles.

The Inca gods were an important part of everyday life. They were often connected to the living world of plants, animals, and the landscape—mountains, in particular. Because the Inca believed that gods controlled the rains and harvests, they wanted to keep them happy with prayers and sacrificial offerings of food, drink, and sometimes animals.

This idea of giving back to the living landscape was an important part of Inca life, and everyone made daily offerings to ensure health and happiness for their families. The Inca also believed that sometimes the gods wanted more than a cup of beer and a cut of llama meat.

Viracocha: The supreme god of the Incas, he created the earth, heavens, sun, moon, and all living things.

Inti: The sun god, he brings the warmth, light, and sunshine needed for growing crops.

Mama Quilla: The goddess of love and marriage and the protector of women.

Pachamama: The fertility goddess, she protects pregnant women and babies, and looks after each year's harvest.

Supay: The god of death and ruler of the underworld.

The most valuable gift the Inca could give the gods was the life of a child. This important decision was made by those in power, and only happened on rare occasions. Perhaps the emperor wanted the gods to bring a rich harvest, or the gods were angry and needed to be soothed. Whatever the reason, the emperor would send agents to the far corners of his empire to find the ideal child to use as an offering.

Around 500 years ago, a girl around the age of 15, who we now call La Doncella (The Maiden), was chosen. There is a lot we don't know about her, like her real name or where she came from. We don't know what she was like as a person, or how she felt about being used as an offering to the gods. What we do know is what happened to her during the final months of her life, and the last moments before her death.

After being chosen, La Doncella was taken to the capital city Cusco to be prepared. There she was treated like royalty. Her old diet of potatoes and vegetables appears to have changed to feasts of meat and maize. She was dressed in the finest clothes, lived in a secluded temple, and took part in religious ceremonies with the emperor himself.

The priests decided when she was ready to go to her place of sacrifice—a mountain called Llullaillaco, 800 miles away. This difficult journey was made on foot and would have taken many months. Wearing a magnificent white feather headdress, La Doncella led a parade of priests, royal officials, and servants from village to village, where feasts, music, and religious rituals were held in her honor. Although treated like a princess, La Doncella would have known that her life would soon be ending.

The last stage was an exhausting hike up the rocky slopes of Llullaillaco, where the air is thin and hard to breathe. La Doncella was given coca leaves to chew (some were found half eaten in her cheek) to stop her from becoming too tired.

We'll never know how she felt as she looked down on the world spread out below. Did she sense the gods watching? Was she proud to have been chosen? Sad to leave her family? Afraid to die? Perhaps all these things. When they reached the summit, the priests performed a solemn ceremony asking the gods to accept this young girl, their most precious gift.

During special ceremonies, the Inca used decorated cups like this to drink from.

After a year of preparation, a 800-mile journey, and a 4-mile-long climb up a freezing mountain, it was time for La Doncella to meet her fate. The priests gave her a strong drink called "chicha," a fermented brew made from maize, which dulled her senses and made her fuzzy-headed. Eventually, the combination of chicha, cold, and exhaustion would have made her fall unconscious. The priests then wrapped a cloth around her head to stop her from breathing . . . and waited.

Starved of oxygen, La Doncella appears to have slipped from sleep into death. She was then sealed inside a chamber in the ground wearing her feather headdress, ready for the gods to receive her.

To end a child's life is a terrible thing to do, but the Inca didn't see it this way. They believed that even though her heart had stopped, she was not really dead. La Doncella still lived, roaming free in the mountains, watching over and protecting her people for eternity. Her passing into the gods' care was a cause of celebration, not sorrow.

La Doncella was one of three child sacrifices found on the mountain. Each child—two girls and a boy—had been buried in a tomb dug into the ground. The Inca priests left many precious objects alongside the children, including jewelry, gold statuettes, and food offerings. There were also beautiful dolls, complete with feather headdresses and colorful woven costumes.

CT scans allowed scientists to look through La Doncella's clothes and skin at her bones and soft tissues. As well as her finely woven alpaca tunic, the cold had preserved her body so completely that her organs were intact and there was blood in her veins—even her last breath of air was still trapped in her lungs.

The Chinchorro Mummies

Thousands of years before the ancient Egyptians built the Great Pyramid at Giza, another desert-dwelling people on the other side of the world were already mummifying their dead. They lived in small groups, hunting on the land, fishing in the sea, and creating the oldest mummies in the world.

The Chinchorro lived on the west coast of South America. From 7000 BC their culture survived for over 5,500 years before fading away around 1500 BC. They lived in small groups on a narrow strip of fertile land between the rolling waves of the Pacific Ocean and the endless sands of the Atacama Desert.

The sea provided most of their food; the Chinchorro hunted sea lions for their meat, tusks, and skins, dove for shellfish, and used nets, harpoons, and hooks made from cactus spines to catch fish. Without knowledge of metals or pottery, they instead made tools from stone, animal bones, and seashells. Many of their mummies show signs of an ear disease called "external auditory exostoses," an abnormal bone growth within the ear canal probably caused by regularly diving in cold water.

Cactus spines or shells could be used to make fishing hooks, and long spears called harpoons were used to catch large fish.

Fishermen's Tackle

Items left with the mummies (called "grave goods") reflect the Chinchorro's reliance on the sea to provide most of their food. They include fishing equipment such as hooks, weighted nets, and tools to pry shellfish from rocks.

As far as we know, the Chinchorro were the first people in history to mummify their dead. The three methods they used—called the black, red, and mud techniques—needed patience, skill, and a good knowledge of the human body. The mummies unearthed by archaeologists from the sand include those of men, women, children, the elderly, and even babies who died before they were born. This suggests that the Chinchorro gave the same care and treatment after death to everyone, no matter who or how old they were.

The Chinchorro didn't bury their dead as soon as they were mummified. Many mummies show signs of repainting and repair, revealing that they were kept above ground and among the living for years. Like many cultures, the Chinchorro believed that the spirits of their dead ancestors remained a present and important part of everyday life. Mummies were physical representations of these still-present ancestors, and could be visited whenever friends and relatives wished.

It appears that the dead were considered far too important by the Chinchorro to be hidden away, and people were kept within their community even after their life had ended. Perhaps the Chinchorro believed that the dead had some sort of spiritual power that could be shared if they were kept nearby. Or it might simply have been that the living were comforted by having their loved ones close by to look at, talk to, and touch.

Disassembling and Drying the Body

The Chinchorro used a range of mummification techniques over the centuries. For some bodies, the head, limbs, and skin were separated from the body and the remaining soft tissues removed. The arm and leg bones were sometimes dried over a smouldering fire, the body cavity filled with hot coals, and the skull contents replaced with mud and reeds.

Reassembling the Body

Once the skeletal remains had dried, the body was reassembled. Sticks were usually used to reinforce the limbs and spine, and the skull was reattached to the neck. This took days of careful work. Mud or paste made from ash, grass, and sea-lion blood was molded over the skeleton to resemble a person with a body, limbs, and head. Once fully formed, this paste flesh was allowed to dry.

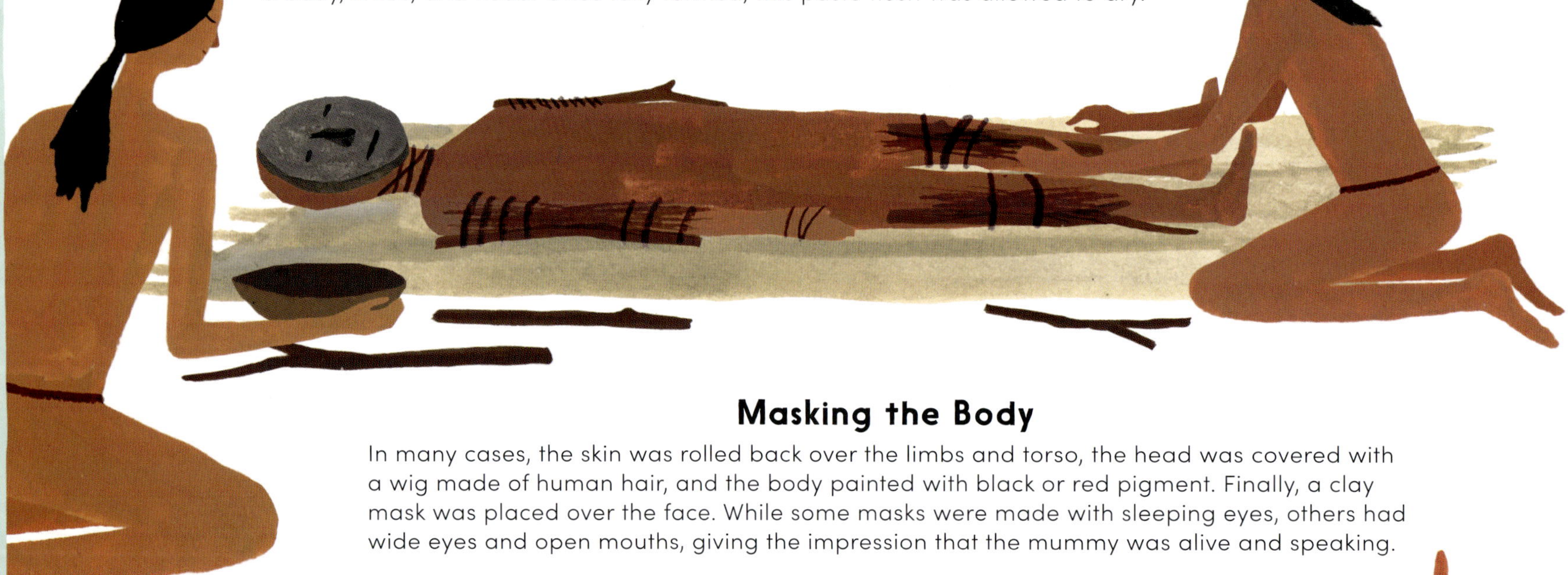

Masking the Body

In many cases, the skin was rolled back over the limbs and torso, the head was covered with a wig made of human hair, and the body painted with black or red pigment. Finally, a clay mask was placed over the face. While some masks were made with sleeping eyes, others had wide eyes and open mouths, giving the impression that the mummy was alive and speaking.

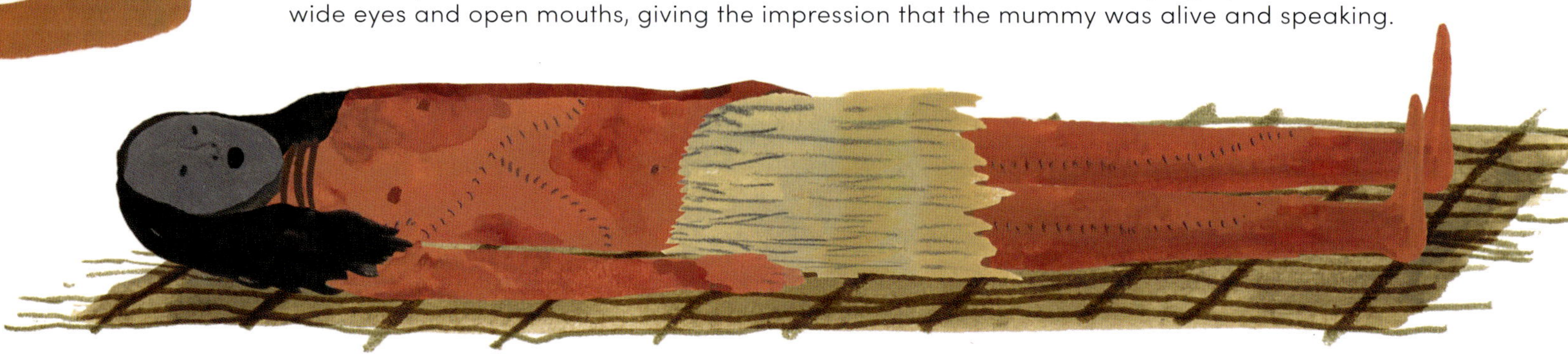

Mud Mummies

Sometimes the Chinchorro used a simpler mummification method. Instead of the complex rebuilding processes of the red and black techniques, the body appears to have been dried out and covered in a thick paste made from mud. This paste coating was molded to look like the person and once it had dried, the mummy was painted and buried.

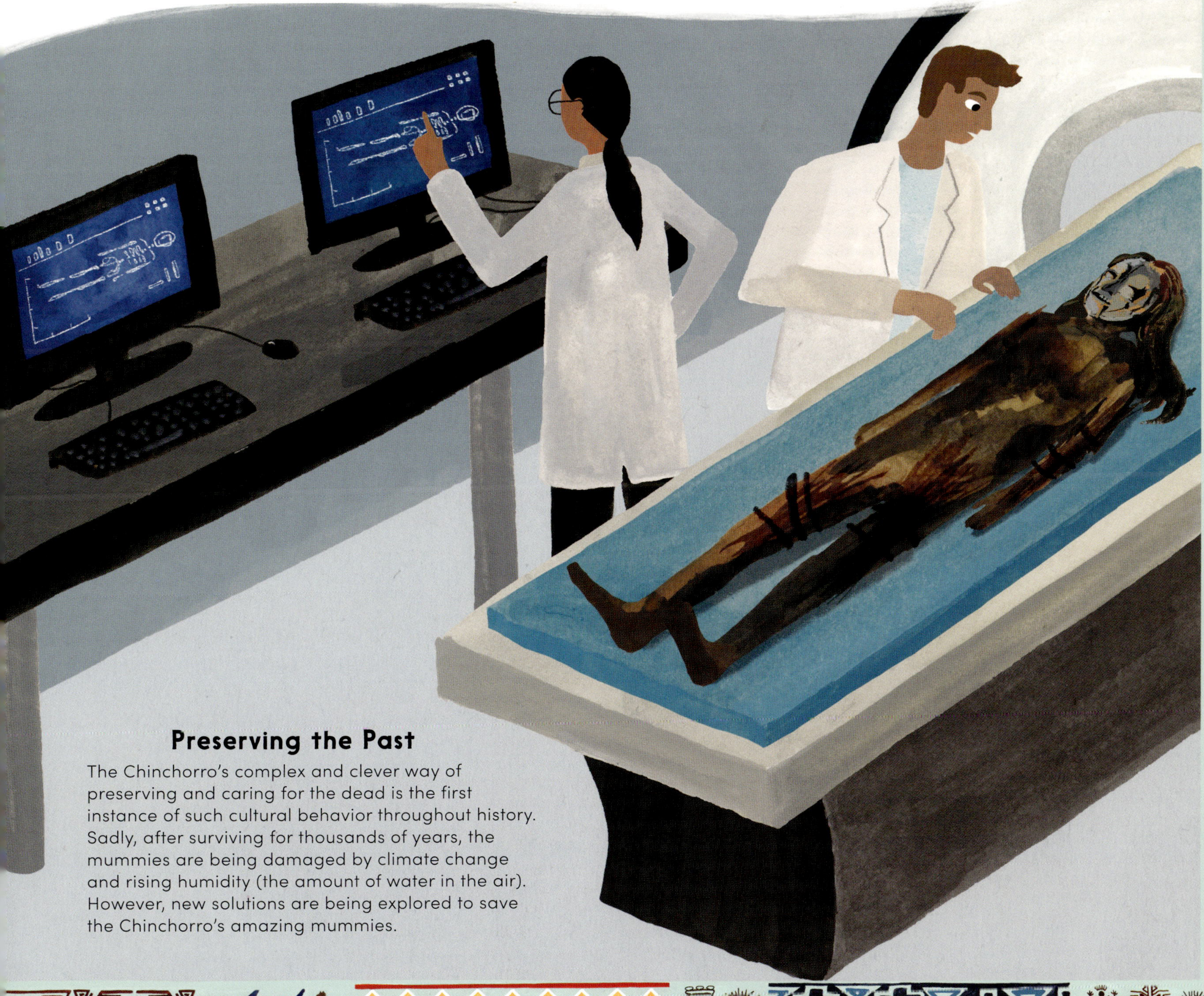

Preserving the Past

The Chinchorro's complex and clever way of preserving and caring for the dead is the first instance of such cultural behavior throughout history. Sadly, after surviving for thousands of years, the mummies are being damaged by climate change and rising humidity (the amount of water in the air). However, new solutions are being explored to save the Chinchorro's amazing mummies.

Franklin's Lost Expedition

In 1845, Sir John Franklin and his crew of 134 men set sail from England on two Royal Navy ships, HMS *Erebus* and HMS *Terror*. Their goal was to discover the Northwest Passage, a sea route across the top of the world from the Atlantic to the Pacific Ocean. Three men died early—some think they were the lucky ones. Last seen sailing into the jagged white teeth of the Canadian Arctic, Franklin and his crew were never heard from again.

By September 1846, Franklin and his men were deep inside an intimidating landscape of rock-strewn islands, towering icebergs, freezing winds, and pack ice drifting on steel-gray seas. The Arctic winter fell, bringing months of never-ending darkness. Ice closed in, trapping both ships in a grip that refused to loosen. Timbers creaked. Cold wind whistled through the cracks. Men sickened and died—including Franklin himself. The crew endured this nightmare for 19 long months until, in desperation, they abandoned ship to attempt a 1,000-mile journey south on foot.

Cold, starving, and exhausted, they dragged their supplies on sleds, but in the end it proved too much. No one survived. The Franklin Expedition was defeated by the place they'd tried to conquer.

Many rescue attempts were made to find the lost expedition, but it wasn't until 1857 that the first bodies of the men who attempted that doomed journey were found. Some of the recovered bones appear to have cut marks on their surface. These were probably made by knives being used to cut away flesh. Many people believe that some men were driven almost mad with hunger and were forced to eat parts of their dead comrades.

This map shows the route Franklin and his men took in their ships.

Three sailors died in the expedition's early months and were buried on a scrap of windswept land called Beechey Island. Perfectly preserved in the permafrost (ground that is always frozen), their bodies provide clues about how they died.

John Torrington was 20, with blue eyes and long brown hair. His lungs were smoke-stained from working with the ship's steam engine. He suffered from tuberculosis, an infectious disease that weakened his muscles and caused fever, night sweats, and coughing fits.

John Hartnell was 25. A Y shaped scar on his body shows that the *Erebus*'s surgeon examined his insides before burial; Franklin probably wanted to know why two of his men had died only four days apart.

William Braine was 32. He was tall and strong, with a curly black beard. Rope burns on his shoulders show that he had been pulling a sled shortly before death. Rats appear to have gnawed his body as he lay below deck, while his comrades hacked out his grave in the frozen ground outside.

Before they died, William and the two Johns had wasted away to skin and bone. Their stomachs were empty, showing that they hadn't eaten a morsel during their final days. Already weak from other sicknesses such as tuberculosis, they seemed to have died from a lung disease called pneumonia. Many of their comrades are likely to have suffered a similar fate months later, during the long, cold death of the Franklin Expedition.

Ötzi the Ice Man

In 1991, high in the mountains of northern Italy that border Austria, some hikers made an extraordinary discovery: the body of a man lying face down on the rocks, his legs still encased in solid ice. He was so well-preserved, the hikers thought he was a mountaineer who had only recently died. But they were wrong. This man was very, very old.

Using radiocarbon dating, scientists discovered he'd died in early summer over 5,000 years ago, during the European Copper Age (3500–1700 BC). Because he'd been found in the Ötzal Alps, they named him Ötzi.

Ötzi had been beautifully preserved in the ice, with his skin, bones and teeth all intact. He had brown hair and eyes, stood at 5.2 feet tall, and was between the ages of 35 and 55 when he died. A diet of coarse grains had eroded his teeth. He suffered from gum disease, wear and tear on his joints, and hardened arteries. Sixty-one tattoos, made by rubbing charcoal into cuts in the skin, covered his body. Years of breathing in smoke from campfires had stained his lungs black.

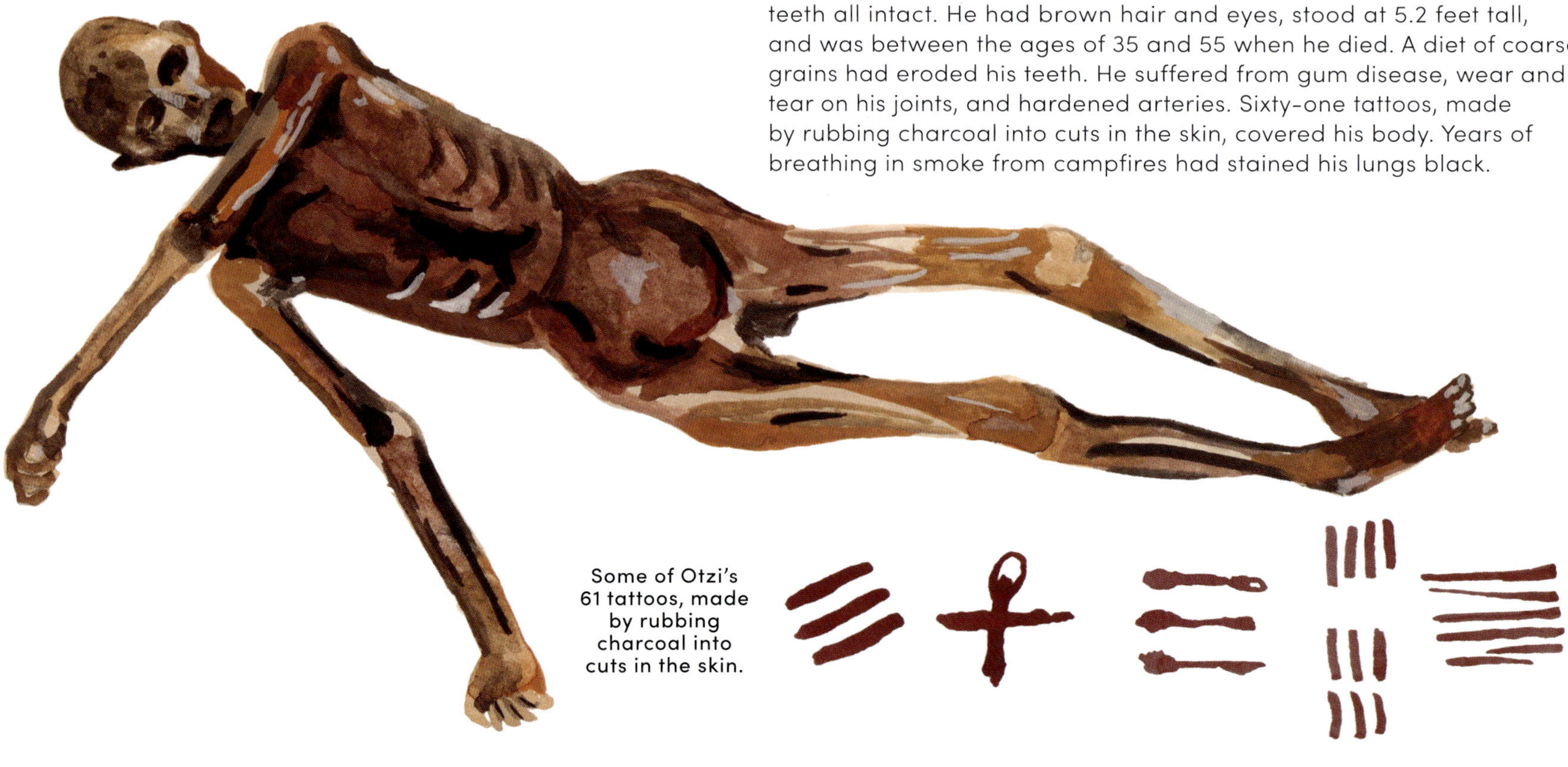

Some of Otzi's 61 tattoos, made by rubbing charcoal into cuts in the skin.

Scientists examined Ötzi's stomach and found a last meal of mountain-goat meat, unleavened (yeast-free) bread, and a type of berry called a sloe. Two hours after eating this food, Ötzi was dead.

Sloe berries

Unleavened bread

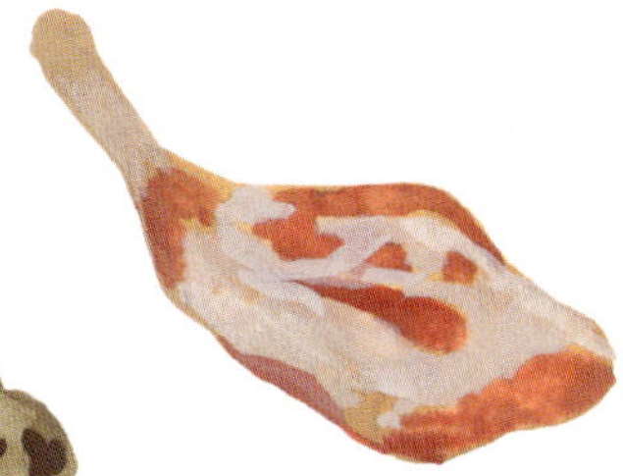

Goat meat

The ice also preserved Ötzi's clothes and possessions. He wore sheepskin leggings and coat, a bear-fur hat, and lace-up cow and ox-hide shoes insulated with grass. These repairable and well-made clothes would have kept Ötzi warm and dry.

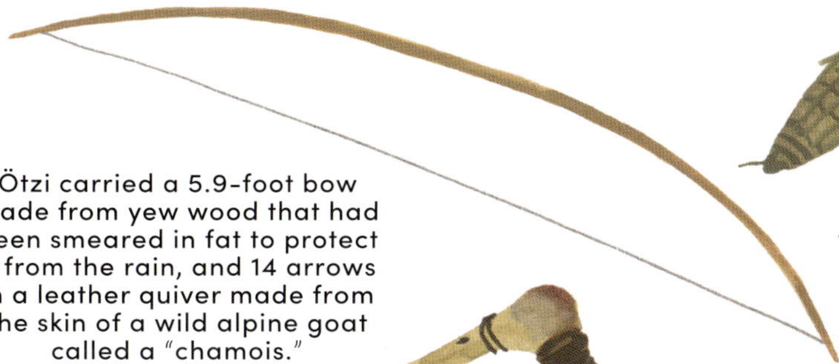

Ötzi carried a 5.9-foot bow made from yew wood that had been smeared in fat to protect it from the rain, and 14 arrows in a leather quiver made from the skin of a wild alpine goat called a "chamois."

Inside a grass-woven sheath was a flint knife.

Ötzi's prize possession was a high-quality copper-headed axe with a yew wood handle.

With his trusty tool-making, fire-lighting, and medicine kits, Ötzi had everything he needed to survive in the alpine landscape he called home. So why did this well-equipped man die alone so far up in the mountains?

At first, scientists thought Ötzi had died from the cold, but further investigation made them realize his death was far more complicated. A stone arrowhead lodged in his left shoulder proves that someone shot him from behind. Wounded and bleeding, it's likely he bled to death. Deep cuts on his right hand suggest he had been injured in a fight a day or so before he died. Were those cuts caused by the same person who later shot him with the arrow?

We will never know who killed Ötzi, or their motive for doing so, but his icy preservation and lucky discovery means that scientists could analyze his remains and reveal extraordinary insights about his life—and death—from over 5,000 years ago.

The Plaster Citizens of Pompeii

One day in the year 79 AD, the people of Pompeii—a bustling coastal town in the heart of the Roman Empire—were overcome by tragedy. For years they had lived there, never giving much thought to the green-sloped mountain lurking a few miles away. By the end of that terrible day, Pompeii had been utterly destroyed and the citizens entombed under layers of ash spewed from that very mountain. This is the story of their death and rediscovery.

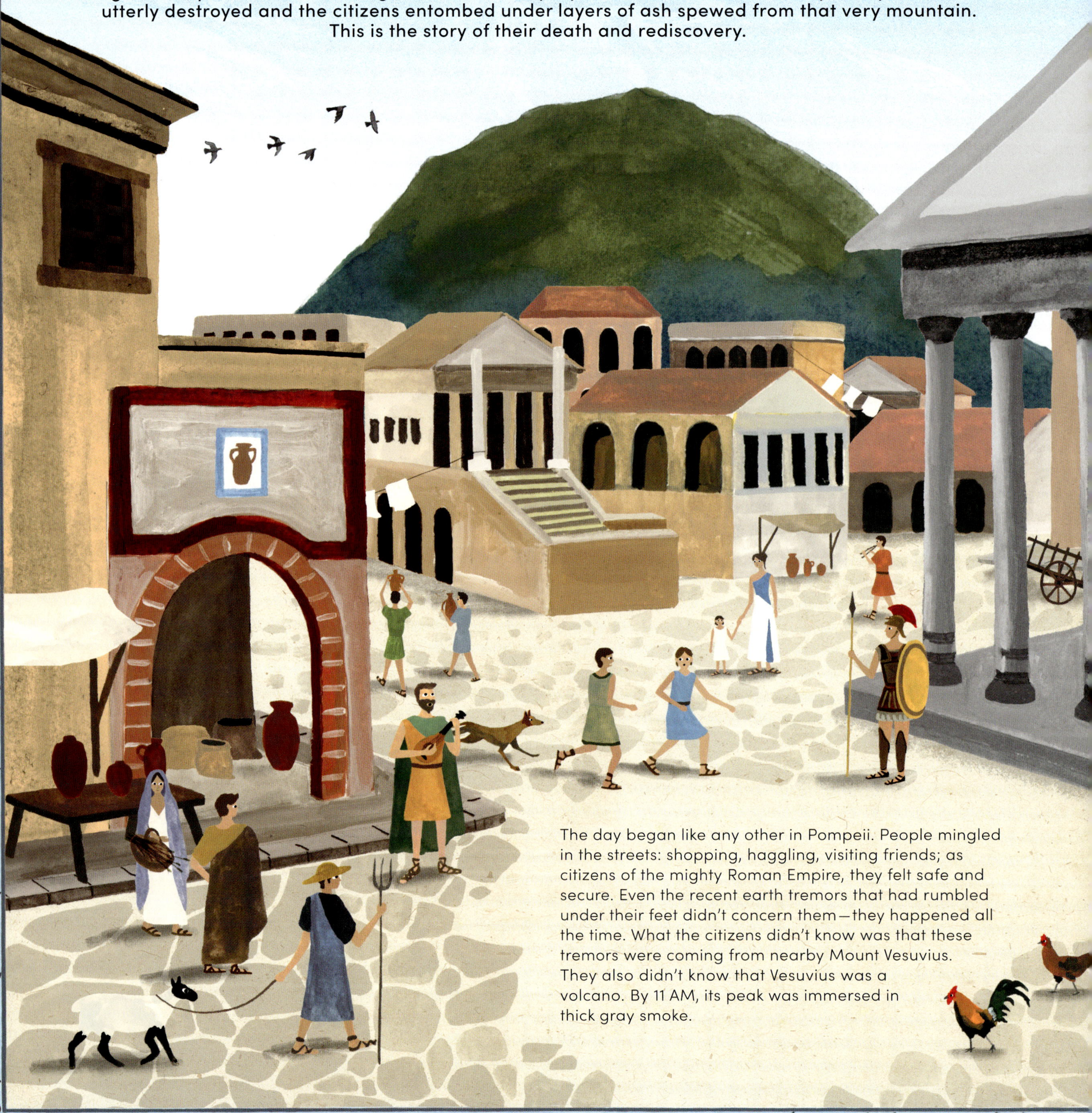

The day began like any other in Pompeii. People mingled in the streets: shopping, haggling, visiting friends; as citizens of the mighty Roman Empire, they felt safe and secure. Even the recent earth tremors that had rumbled under their feet didn't concern them—they happened all the time. What the citizens didn't know was that these tremors were coming from nearby Mount Vesuvius. They also didn't know that Vesuvius was a volcano. By 11 AM, its peak was immersed in thick gray smoke.

At around noon, the molten (liquid) rock that had been building up beneath the volcano, burst out in a catastrophic explosion. Citizens stared, horror-struck, as a column of smoke and ash rose 12 miles up into the sky. They staggered and screamed as the first shockwave hit their town, cracking walls and shaking buildings. The mountain—where for years they'd grazed sheep and grown grapes to make wine—had burst into furious life.

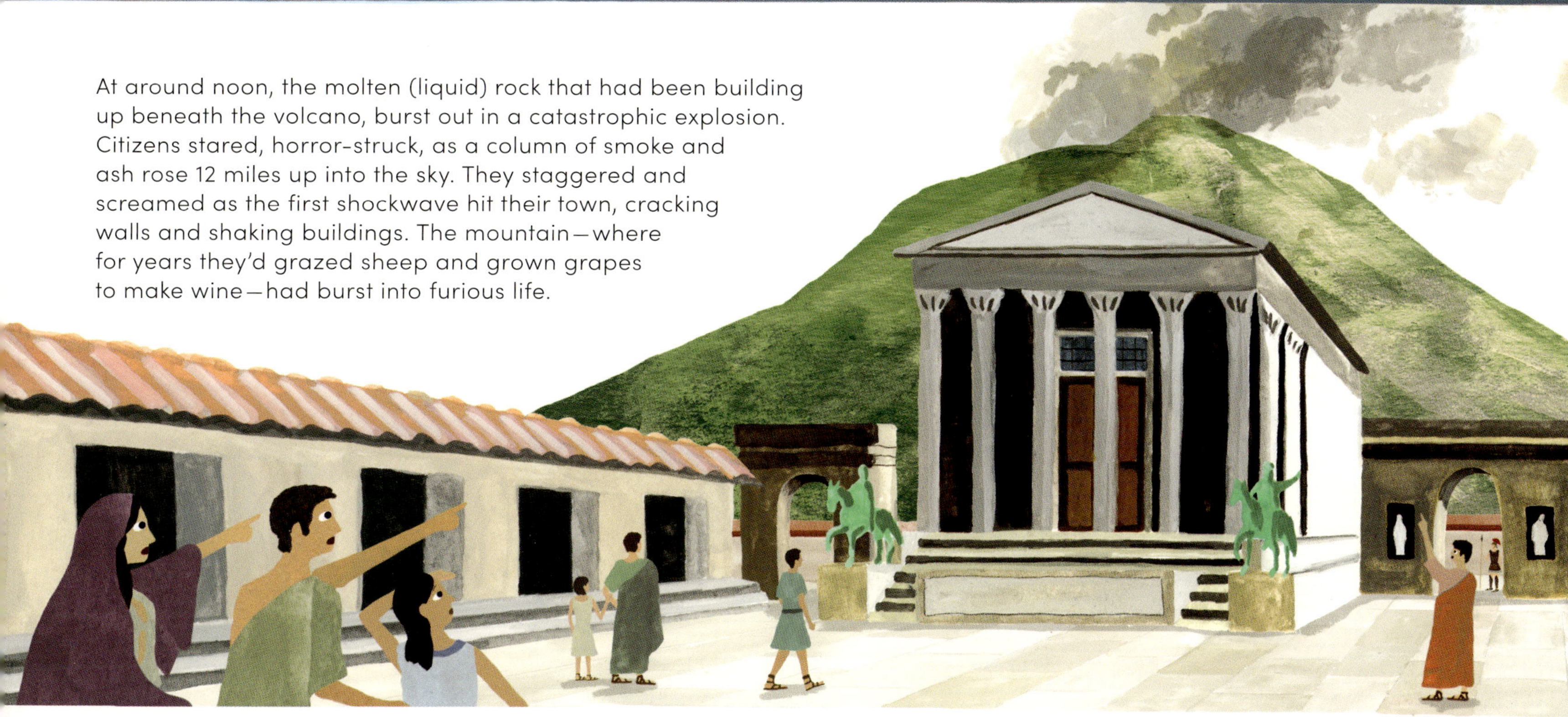

Smoke spread over their heads, turning the sky black at a frightening speed. The sun disappeared. Hot ash fell within minutes, choking, burning, and smothering every surface. It piled into drifts, clogged doors, filled courtyards, and poured through windows. Burning rocks traveling at high speed shattered roofs and started countless fires. To the panicked citizens of Pompeii, it must have felt as if their world was ending.

The world had turned pitch-black. Ash and rocks fell for hours. Citizens huddled under stairs or in cellars. The heat was intense, the air unbreathable.

By 11 PM, the dense black column suspended over the volcano was 17 miles high; millions of tons of ash, held in the air by the intense heat, gathered above the volcano's gaping mouth. As the temperature cooled, the column collapsed under its own immense weight. This was the end for Pompeii.

Surviving citizens had no idea that super-heated air, volcanic gas, rocks, and ash were avalanching down the volcano's slopes and hurtling toward them. Barreling along at 65 miles per hour, these roaring gray waves swallowed and smashed everything in their path. Anyone left in Pompeii was instantly killed and buried under feet of ash. By dawn, Pompeii and her people had disappeared.

Ancient Romans Recreated

Vesuvius destroyed and preserved Pompeii. The ash that emerged from it kept the streets, buildings, and people undisturbed for 1,700 years. Now, after decades of excavation, we can explore the town in the shadow of the volcano, just as the ancient Romans did, and examine the bodies they left behind.

When Italian archaeologist Giuseppe Fiorelli found cavities in the hardened ash in the 1860s, he realized they'd been created by people buried during the disaster. Their bodies had mostly decomposed, leaving nothing behind except bones and an empty void. Giuseppe filled these voids with liquid plaster. Once dried, it created perfect casts of people at their moment of death.

Plaster Animals

Animals died, too. This guard dog was left tied to a post inside a front door. It tried to clamber up the growing ash piles until the leash around its neck stopped it from climbing any higher.

The intimate details captured in the plaster bring us close to the citizens of Pompeii. We can examine the folds in their clothing, the sandals on their feet; we can see their faces, even their final expressions. Some Pompeiians had fractured skulls, which may have been caused by falling rocks or the intense heat. Others huddled indoors, covering their faces against the choking ash, or holding loved ones close. Many tried to escape the ever-rising ash by clambering on to rooftops. It made no difference where they went—the citizens who stayed in the town were doomed.

House of Green Bones

Excavations in the late 20th century uncovered the skeletons of 54 Pompeiians who'd sought refuge in a large stone warehouse. Men, women, and children had waited in the darkness as the ground trembled and hot ash fell outside. Studying their bones tells us how these people died and, perhaps more importantly, how they lived.

The skeletons' positions indicate that when the people arrived in the warehouse they divided themselves into two groups. One had no possessions except the clothes they wore, the other carried bags of gold coins and jewelry. The rich group's precious metals reacted with the ash, and over time stained their bones green. Among the rich was a girl with silver earrings, and an elderly man with a child on his lap.

Finding the remains of rich and poor together allowed scientists to compare them. The poor people's skeletons were similar to those of the rich, with little sign of disease, showing that most Pompeiians enjoyed a relatively healthy life and benefited from a balanced diet of meat, fish, and vegetables. Roman poor—in Pompeii at least—appear to have been relatively healthy. The adults' teeth show a lot of wear due to the grit in their diet, possibly from the bread they ate.

The skeletons in the cellar bear many scars caused by the volcano's fury. Intense heat burned away the soft tissue, and speeding fire particles left black marks on skulls and bones. Luckily, death was almost instantaneous.

The Capuchin Catacombs

Beneath the stone floor of the Capuchin monastery in Palermo, Sicily, are a series of halls, corridors, and chambers now dimly lit with electric lights. The air is dusty and dry. Hanging from the walls, standing in recesses, and lying in lidless coffins are hundreds of mummies—men, women, and children—all fully dressed and on display. Who were they, and how did they end up here?

When Capuchin monks dug up the bodies of some of their deceased fellow monks at the end of the 16th century, they were amazed at how well-preserved they were. Convinced this was the work of God, they moved the mummies to a new room inside their monastery. More deceased friars were stored over the following decades, usually wearing robes, and the Capuchin catacombs were made bigger to accommodate them.

After a while the monks offered their mummification and display service to anyone who could afford it. This meant that friends and family could visit their loved ones whenever they wanted, safe in the knowledge that the monks would look after them and even wash and change their clothes to keep them looking fresh.

Bodies destined to be put on display were first taken to a preparation room called the *colatoio*. They were then laid on a grid made from terracotta tubes (terracotta is a type of pottery) and left to dry out, or "desiccate," for about a year. This left them stiff but with skin and hair intact. The bodies were then washed with vinegar, occasionally stuffed with straw and bay leaves, and finally, dressed up and placed in their new home inside the Capuchin Catacombs.

Perhaps the most famous mummy in the catacombs belongs to a girl named Rosalia Lombardo. She was only two years old when she died of pneumonia in 1920. Heartbroken, her father asked a professional embalmer named Alfredo Salafia to use his expertise to preserve her body.

Alfredo set to work. He used a special embalming fluid called "Alfredo Salafia's Protection Fluid: New Special Formula for the Preservation of the Entire Human Cadaver in a Permanently Fresh State," that he'd invented himself. Ingredients included formalin to kill decay-causing bacteria, salicylic acid to kill fungi, glycerin to stop the flesh and skin from shriveling, and zinc salts to ensure the body kept its natural shape. This mixture was injected and allowed to spread throughout Rosalia's body.

Alfredo's procedure worked so well that, over 100 years later, Rosalia's state of preservation is almost miraculous: her brain and organs are intact and in place, her skin is tight and unmarked, and her flesh plump. She doesn't look dead, only dozing—perhaps this helped to comfort her grieving father.

Bog Bodies

For the people of the European Iron Age, wetlands and peat bogs were a source of fuel, wild food, and basket-making materials. They were also dangerous. Even where there were wooden trackways it was treacherous finding a path through, and many people were led astray by the ghostly light of a will-o'-the-wisp to drown in hidden pools. Is this why so many ancient bodies have been found in these strange, misty places? Or is there an even darker reason for their deaths?

The raised peat bogs of northern Europe are special. Waterlogged, covered in grass, moss, and reeds, they were once lakes that became stagnant after losing their fresh-water supply. Over the centuries, the bogs filled up with layers of partially rotted vegetation, which formed into dense peat. Insects and bacteria that normally cause rot cannot live in these oxygen-free bogs, so any submerged animals or people are preserved.

Though acidic water caused by decaying plants dissolves their bones, a chemical mixture created by sphagnum moss preserves hair, skin, and tendons; it also turns skin brown and leathery, and hair red. When such remains are discovered, careful excavation and forensic research provides fantastic evidence about the bodies, their clothing, wooden objects, and basketry, which do not survive in normal archaeological sites.

Tollund Man

Porridge was commonly eaten by Iron Age people during winter, when fresh vegetables were scarce.

Tollund Man was found 6.5 feet deep in a peat bog in Denmark, so well-preserved his discoverers thought he was the victim of a recent murder. In fact, he died sometime between 375 and 210 BC, making him over 2,300 years old. He was naked, except for a belt around his waist and a pointed cap of sheepskin and wool over his head. When he died, Tollund Man was around 30–40 years old and stood at about 5.24 feet tall. His hair was cut close to his scalp, and his chin and upper lip were covered in stubble.

At this time, when a person died, it was normal to hold a funeral ceremony where the body was cremated (burned to ashes in a fire). So why was Tollund Man treated differently? Why did his people leave his body intact and all alone in a bog? The answer might lie in the way he died.

Tollund Man was killed. The evidence for this is the preserved leather noose that was found still knotted around his neck. This suggests he was hanged, perhaps from a tree. Was he murdered? Executed as a criminal? Both could be true, but the way he was treated after his death suggests another explanation.

Tollund Man was laid in his grave with his legs and arms drawn into his body like someone in a deep and comfortable sleep. His people also closed his eyes and mouth (which would have been open after death by hanging), giving him his peaceful expression. Some experts believe it's doubtful they would have treated a common criminal in such a considerate way, suggesting that Tollund Man was left in the bog as a sacrifice to the spirits of the natural world.

The bog preserved Tollund Man's heart, lungs, and liver. His stomach still contained food, eaten around 12 hours before he died. It was a kind of porridge made from wild seeds, barley, flax, and knotgrass.

We will never know Tollund Man's real name, or what he was thinking when he ate his final meal. His life and personality will forever remain a mystery. But when visitors to the Silkeborg Museum in Denmark look at his peaceful face, with its every line and crease so perfectly preserved, they often feel a connection with him, and fall into silent thought.

A noose was found around Tollund Man's neck.

Yde Girl

Yde Girl was found in 1897, buried in peat near the Dutch town of Yde (pronounced "EE-da"). When her discoverers saw her striking red hair, they thought she was a devil and ran away in terror. But who was she really? And what was her life in the Iron Age like?

Yde Girl was a Celt. The Celts lived in Europe from around 1200 BC and shared many customs and religious beliefs. They were farmers, fearsome warriors, and skilled metalworkers. Yde Girl probably lived in a village surrounded by fields, where everyone knew each other. Family life centered around the fire; kept alight 24 hours a day, it provided light, heat, cooked food, and comfort.

Although the Celts' way of life was different from ours, like all people past and present, they loved and looked after each other. Despite this, at some point during Yde Girl's 16th year, she was killed and left in a bog, possibly by the very people who had known her and watched her grow up.

One explanation is that Yde Girl was chosen to be a human sacrifice. She was possibly given to the spirit world sometime between 54 BC and 128 AD, wrapped in a cloak and with the woolen belt that had strangled her still wrapped around her neck.

At only 4.5 feet tall, she was small for her age. Scans show she had scoliosis, a condition that caused her spine to bend sideways and probably made walking difficult. Long forgotten before her discovery, a facial reconstruction now gives us a good idea of what this young girl might have looked like before her untimely end.

Clonycavan Man and Old Croghan Man

The bogs of Ireland contain more than just peat. Weapons, jewelry, and even wooden tubs of Iron-Age butter have been unearthed from their soggy depths. People have been found too, caked in mud and secrets.

Clonycavan Man was around 20 years old when he died sometime between 392 and 201 BC. A short man, it's possible he styled his nit-infested hair into a pile on top of his head to make him look taller. The hair was kept in place with the Iron-Age equivalent of hair gel—a sticky mixture of plant oil and pine-tree resin.

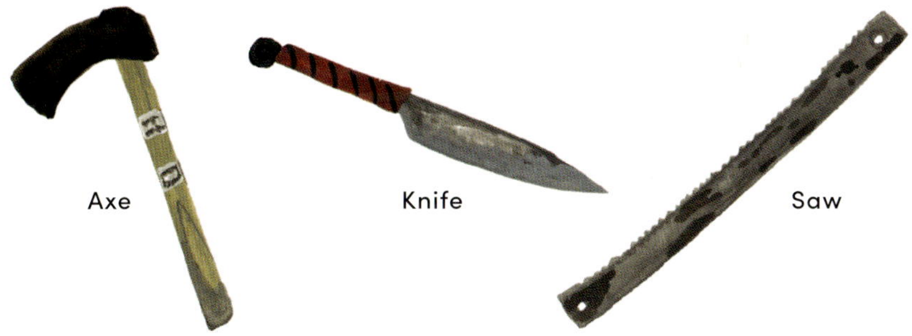

In life, Old Croghan Man stood at an imposing 6.43 feet. All that's left of him is a leathery torso and two arms. Well-kept nails and good health at the time of his death (between 362 and 175 BC) indicates he was someone of wealth and importance.

Clonycavan Man's head was hit three times with an axe, splitting his skull almost in two. His killers also stabbed him and cut his abdomen (belly) open. Old Croghan Man was killed by a knife in the chest. A cut on his upper arm shows he faced his killer and tried to deflect the strike. After death, his head was cut off and his body sawn in half. It's possible these men were unpopular leaders, violently executed by their vengeful subjects, but the lack of evidence makes this uncertain. All we know is that you can strip a bog body of mud, but not of mystery.

Lindow Man

Bog bodies give us a remarkable glimpse of the people who lived during the European Iron Age. Scientific experiments can reveal many things about them, but the picture is never complete.

Lindow Man was discovered buried in a peat bog called Lindow Moss in Cheshire, England. His remains consist of a head, a flattened torso, both arms, and parts of both legs. His facial features are clear to see despite being distorted by the weight of the peat. Bog acid has turned his flesh to leather by a chemical process called "tanning," making it soft and preserving the skin's natural lines and wrinkles.

After being dug up, Lindow Man was taken to the British Museum to be looked after. Tests showed that he died sometime between 2 BC and 119 AD, meaning he could have been alive during the Iron Age or the later Romano-British period that began when the ancient Romans conquered Britain.

Lindow Man was a healthy 25-year-old when he died, standing at 5.5 feet tall and weighing around 140 pounds. He had a mustache and a short, neatly trimmed beard. The preserved contents of Lindow Man's stomach included a last meal of unleavened bread, and an infestation of whipworm—a parasite that lives inside human intestines.

Armband made of fox fur

We don't know how Lindow Man made a living, but his fingernails are neat, which suggests it didn't involve manual labor. Perhaps he was a leader or a wealthy merchant. We don't know why he's naked except for a fox-fur armband. It's possible he was buried nude, or his clothes rotted away in the bog.

We cannot be sure about the details of Lindow Man's death, although we know it was violent. A V-shaped hole in his head was probably caused by an axe. The blow drove pieces of skull into his brain but did not kill him.

He probably died from a neck injury, but how it happened is debatable. Some experts believe the rope found around his throat was a garrotte—a weapon used to strangle— which the killer tightened so much it broke Lindow Man's neck. Others think the rope was only a necklace, and it was a hard strike to the back of the head that killed him.

We know his killers left him face down in the chilly pools of Lindow Moss. Was he left for dead by robbers who ran away? Was he himself a criminal who did not deserve a respectful burial? Or was he sacrificed to spirits of nature?

We can ask many questions, but the answers are often
We don't know; We cannot be sure; Perhaps this; Maybe that.
Bog bodies are mysterious and keep their secrets close.

The Salt Men of Iran

For thousands of years, before the invention of refrigeration, salt was used to preserve meat and fish. This made salt so valuable it was called "white gold," and nations grew rich from the miners who delved underground to hack it out with hammer and pick. Some of these miners have been discovered in an ancient salt mine in Iran, naturally mummified by the very substance they were digging for.

Salt mining in ancient Iran (550 BC–651 AD, then called Persia) was dangerous. Miners worked in dark tunnels, hacking out rock salt with iron picks and chisels. Salt dust caused constant thirst, and the air was hot and dry. Perhaps worst of all was the constant, nagging fear that the tunnels could cave in at any moment.

The first Salt Man was discovered in 1993 after lying undisturbed for 1,700 years in a tunnel that had collapsed and killed him. What remained of this man, who was around 40 years old, was a head, part of his body, and a leg. Just like the natron used by the ancient Egyptians, the salt in the mine dried and preserved his corpse.

Salt Man 1's skull is intact and covered in flesh and skin. His beard and flowing hair had been brown, until chemical changes after death turned them white.

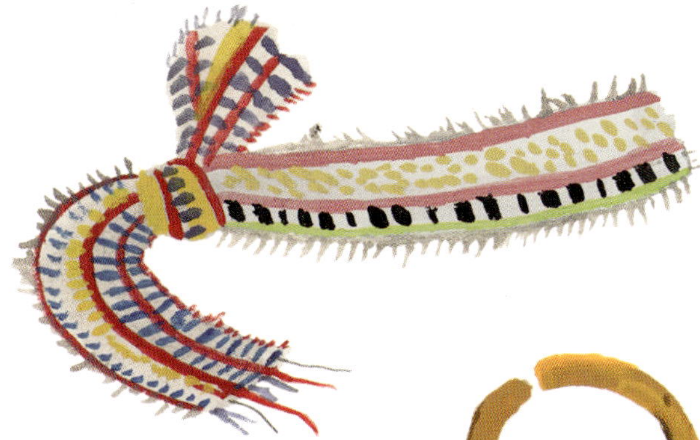

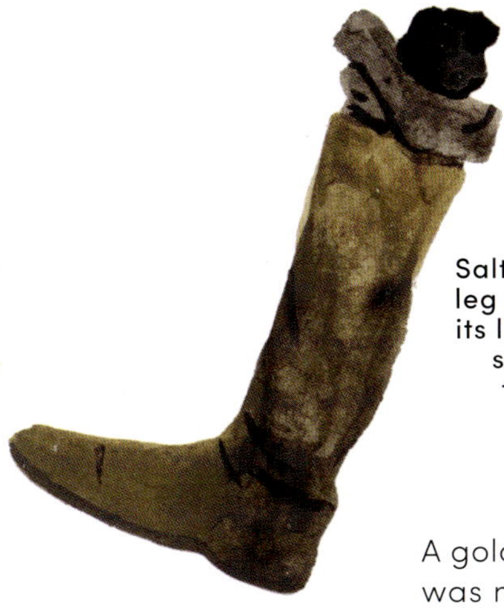

Salt Man 1's left leg is still inside its leather boot, severed at the knee.

Some woven fabric was also found with the men.

Salt Man 1 was wearing a gold earring.

A gold earring and his high-quality boots suggest that Salt Man 1 was not an ordinary miner. What was this wealthy man doing underground in a dust-clogged mine? Was he a visiting salt merchant? Or an administrator inspecting the shafts and tunnels? Whatever the truth, his decision to explore that day proved fatal.

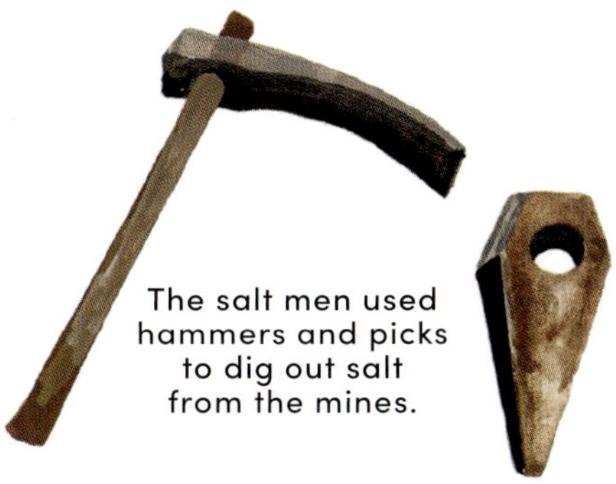

The salt men used hammers and picks to dig out salt from the mines.

Like Salt Man 1, Salt Man 4 died when the mine ceiling fell in on him. But Salt Man 4 was a miner and only 16 years old when, around 330 BC, falling salt blocks crushed his chest and heart. He was 5.41 feet tall and clean-shaven, with short brown hair and a silver hooped earring.

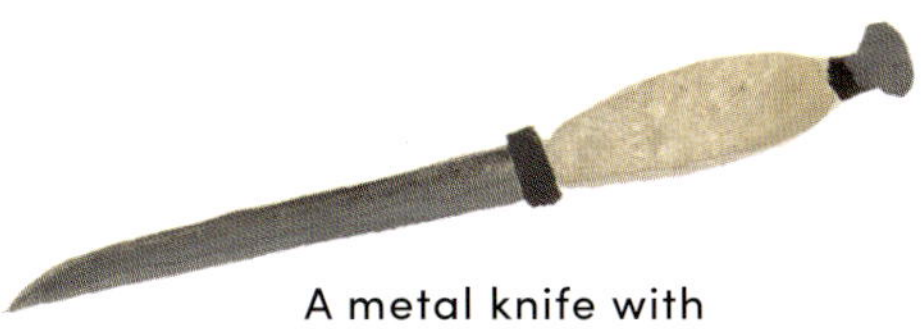

A metal knife with a bone handle was tucked into Salt Man 4's belt.

He wore pants, a brown woolen tunic, and a red cloak made from animal skin.

Salt Man 4 was carrying two pitchers, possibly of drinking water, when he died.

His pose appears to show his last moment: lying on his back, arms held up to protect his head from the tumbling salt blocks. This is misleading. Salt Man 4 actually died face down with one leg tucked up into his chest; perhaps he was trying to run away.

Beauty of Xiaohe

The Taklamakan Desert in western China is a trackless wilderness of shifting sand dunes, wind-carved rocks, burning-hot days, and freezing-cold nights. Deep inside this bleak yet beautiful landscape is an ancient burial ground. It's a strange place, rising from the sand like an island lost in a golden sea. Beneath it lie hundreds of bodies, one of which is regarded as the most beautiful mummy in the world.

Xiaohe (which means "little river" and is pronounced she-ow-HUH) Cemetery is a human-made sand mound covering an area of 0.62 acres. One hundred and forty posts made from poplar wood stick up from the mound, which from a distance looks like the ruins of an ancient hill fort.

Each post marks a grave, the oldest of which was dug around 4,000 years ago. Tall, torpedo-shaped posts mark female graves; shorter, flattened, oar-shaped posts mark male graves. Archaeological excavations have revealed around 330 burials. The cemetery fell into disuse around 400 AD.

Felt hat

Decorative mask

Boot made of fur and leather

Other items were found lying half-buried in the sand: felt hats; leather boots; broken coffins; long-nosed masks with grinning mouths, and eerie figures carved from trees, scattered around like sun-bleached driftwood.

Beneath the posts are boat-shaped coffins made from heavy wooden planks. Many had been sealed with ox skins. Bloodstains on these coffins suggest that the animals were killed and skinned during the burials. It's possible this was done as an animal sacrifice as well as to seal the coffin.

One excavated body is particularly well-preserved. Buried sometime between 1800 and 1500 BC, the warm desert air dried out her body and, along with salty soil and freezing temperatures during the winter, kept her virtually intact for centuries. Her thick hair, striking cheekbones, symmetrical features, and deep-set eyes with long lashes earned her the name "Beauty of Xiaohe."

She was dressed in string undergarments, then wrapped in a white woolen cloak adorned with tassels. On her head was placed a tall white hat made of felt and decorated with feathers, and on her feet were well-made leather boots lined with animal fur. Expertly woven straw baskets containing wheat grains, twigs, flower stems, and an herbal medicine called "ephedra" were placed alongside her, perhaps for use after she passed into the next life. Her coffin also contained the world's oldest cheese—an incredible discovery considering how quickly dairy products usually decay. Made by combining milk with bacteria and yeast, it would have looked and tasted a bit like cottage cheese.

The baskets found alongside Beauty of Xiaohe were intricately woven from straw and filled with wheat, twigs, and herbs.

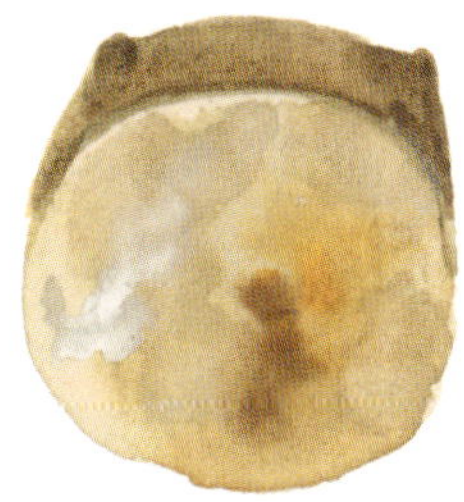

The cheese discovered in the coffin is over 4,000 years old.

So who were these people who built this unique resting place for their dead? Archaeologists believe they settled in the area some 4,000 years ago. At that time, it was not just desert—there were rivers, lakes, trees, animals, and birds. One puzzle about the cemetery is its isolation. There's no evidence of any nearby settlements, and it's thought that the dead were transported long distances by boat, on rivers long since dried up. Why did they choose such a faraway place? Like Beauty of Xiaohe's real name, that will remain a secret.

Lady Xin Zhui

Lady Xin Zhui died and was buried in 163 BC. Ancient Egyptians were still preserving their dead at this time, but where their mummies are now dry husks, Xin Zhui still has soft flesh, flexible skin, and blood-filled veins; her muscles still move, her limbs bend, and every organ is intact. What caused this ancient Chinese noblewoman to be so well-preserved?

Xin Zhui lived during the ancient Chinese Han Dynasty (206 BC–220 AD), a golden period of cultural, technological, and economic development. As a wealthy member of the ruling class, Xin Zhui led a life of luxurious extravagance. An army of servants saw to her every need, and each day she feasted on rich food. When she died at the age of around 50, she was overweight and in poor health.

Xin Zhui's body is over 2,000 years old, but its condition is similar to someone who has only recently died: her skin, flesh, and muscles are moist; her hair, eardrums, and eyelashes intact. Scientific examinations revealed that she suffered from heart disease and bad blood circulation—conditions created by a fat-rich diet and lack of exercise. Bones in her spine had fused together, causing great pain and forcing her to walk with a stick. Undigested melon seeds in her stomach indicate that she died—probably from a heart attack—less than three hours after eating them.

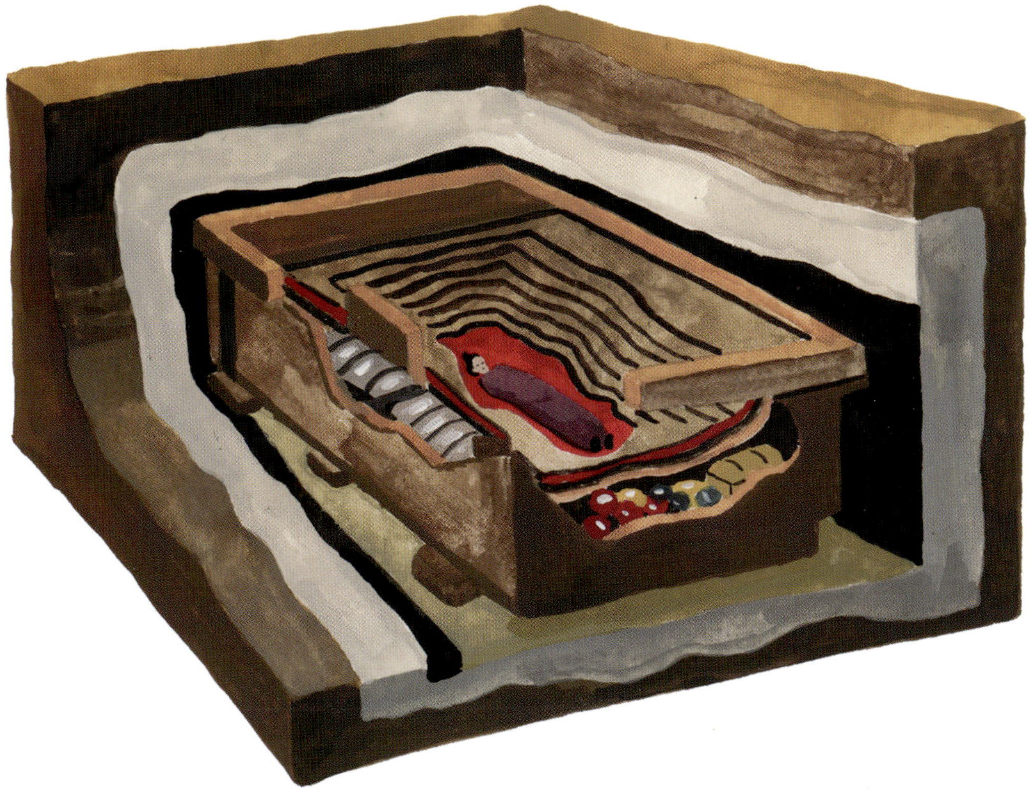

The coffin was covered with a silk funeral banner, showing Xin Zhui preparing to enter the afterlife.

Xin Zhui received a lavish and expensive burial. After being washed, her body was dressed in robes, wrapped in 20 layers of silk, and laid in the smallest of four painted and varnished coffins, one fitting inside the other. These four "nesting" coffins were then lowered into a wood-lined burial chamber 39 feet underground. The chamber was sealed with a wooden roof and bamboo mats, then covered in layers of sand, charcoal, clay, and soil. Scientists believe it was this tomb design that ensured Xin Zhui's body didn't decompose; the water-and-air-tight layers protected her body from decay-causing bacteria, which led to her remarkable preservation.

Lady Xin Zhui's make-up would have been made by boiling and fermenting plants, spices, and animal fats.

Beautiful silk robes were found folded inside her tomb.

As well as baskets of food, Lady Xin Zhui was buried with recipes of her favorite meals.

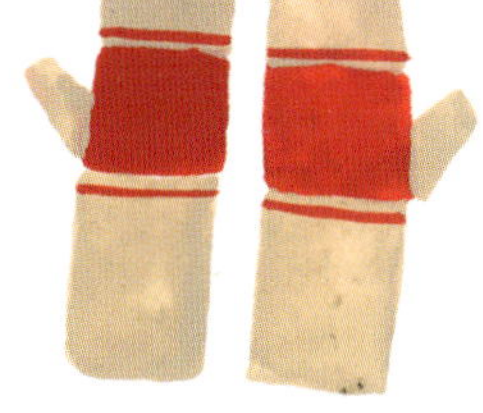

The fingerless mittens found in the tomb were made from expensive silk.

Xin Zhui's tomb was packed with over 1,000 items, including silk robes, fingerless mittens, make-up boxes, musical instruments, plates, bowls, and vases. A huge variety of food was placed in carefully labeled bamboo containers: strawberries, pears, dates, plums, pork, venison, beef, lamb, hare, dog, goose, duck, chicken, turtledove, pheasant, sparrow, fish, eggs, and even owl; Xin Zhui would eat as well in death as she had in life.

The Wet Mummy

The ancient Chinese did not prepare their dead to ensure preservation like the Egyptians or Chinchorro. They did not remove any organs or dry out the flesh before burial. Despite this, ancient Chinese mummies do exist, and are among the best preserved in the world. Scientists believe this is due to the way these bodies were buried, and perhaps the effect of a mysterious fluid found inside their graves.

In 2011, while digging up a road, Chinese workers discovered a small tomb buried 6.5 feet underground. Inside was a solidly constructed coffin made with three layers of wood. When archaeologists opened the lid, they saw bundles of silk and linen submerged in a strange, reddish-brown liquid.

When they peeled back the layers of material, they were astonished to find themselves looking at a near-perfectly preserved woman. Her face, though discolored and blotchy, was still lifelike, filled out, and fully formed. With her closed eyes and peaceful expression, she looked as if she was in a deep sleep, not someone who had died centuries ago.

A coin was found placed on the chest of the mummy to protect against evil spirits in the afterlife.

This 5-foot-tall woman's traditional clothes and pointy shoes were made in a style dating back to the Ming Dynasty, a period of ancient Chinese history that lasted from 1368–1644 AD. This means her mummy could be anywhere between 400 and 700 years old. Scientists haven't determined why she died or what age she was, but her unlined face suggests she was not an old woman.

Beneath a close-fitting cap, her black hair was held in place by a bright silver pin—a typical adornment worn by Ming Dynasty women. Far more striking was the beautiful jade ring on her middle finger. Her jewelry and well-made clothes of quality silk and cotton indicate that she was wealthy, but not a member of the ruling class—perhaps the wife of a merchant or government official.

The Wet Mummy was discovered wearing a close-fitting cap.

Women in the Ming Dynasty often wore hair pins with elaborate carvings on them.

Jade is an expensive green mineral that was popular in ancient China and often used in jewelry.

The Wet Mummy's remarkable preservation is probably due to a combination of things: the tomb was buried deep enough to keep the body permanently cool, and the coffin was filled with an anaerobic (low-oxygen) liquid that stopped bacteria from reaching the body and causing it to decompose.

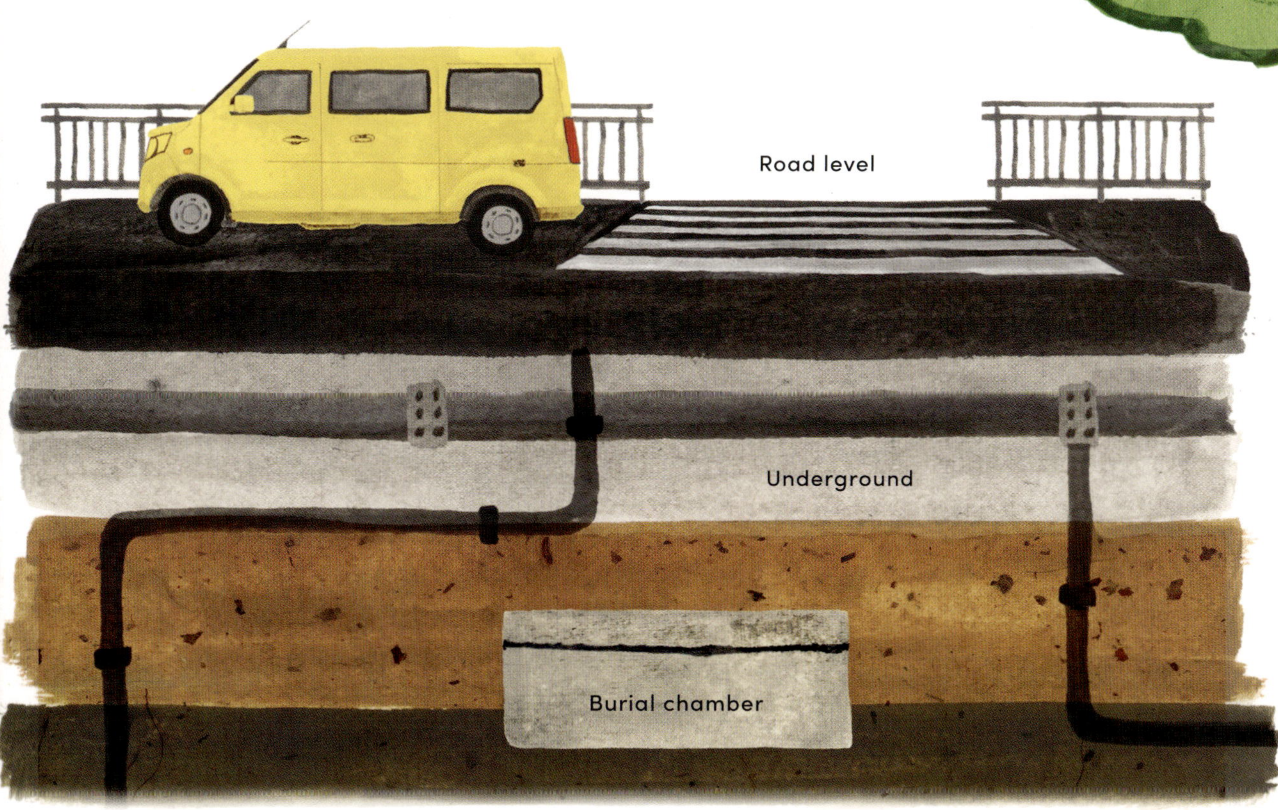

A similar liquid was found inside the graves of other well-preserved ancient Chinese bodies, including Xin Zhui (pages 48–49). Some archaeologists think the ancient Chinese created and poured this liquid into coffins before burial to keep the bodies inside intact. However, most agree it was probably just water that seeped through the wood and reacted with the body to produce a natural embalming fluid.

Painted People of the Steppe

Between 900 and 200 BC, a fierce, warlike people thrived on the plains and grasslands of the vast Siberian steppe. They fought on horseback and lived on the move, never settling in one place for very long. But they were not just warriors: their culture was rich, their craftsmen skilled, especially with gold, and they traded far and wide. These proud horse-lords were called the Scythians (pronounced SIH-thee-uns), and we know much about them from their mummified dead.

Frozen Tombs

The Scythians buried their dead inside tombs called "kurgans"—deep pits with cabin-like structures at the bottom. The coffined body was placed inside the "cabin," along with their most precious possessions. The cabin was sealed with wooden beams, the pit refilled, and a mound of rocks (a "cairn") piled on top.

Objects like cauldrons, flasks, or wooden bowls were lightweight because Scythians lived on the move.

Before burial, the Scythians prepared their dead for the eternal horse ride of the afterlife. The brain was removed through holes bored into the skull; flesh, muscles, and organs were pulled from cuts made in the skin. The body was then packed with straw and hair, and the cuts sewn up with animal tendons (a tough fiber connecting muscles to bones). This process, along with being buried in freezing permafrost, means that some Scythian bodies are remarkably well-preserved even now, 2,500 years later.

The kurgans' secure design and the steppe's permanently freezing temperatures have ensured the survival of thousands of historically priceless Scythian burial goods, including horse harnesses and saddles, carpets, clothing, musical instruments, furniture, cauldrons, cups, weapons, and jewelry. These unique items—some of which are so well-preserved they look as if they were only recently made—give us an intimate view of this ancient culture.

Tantalizingly, there are still many kurgans that have not been examined. What historical art, artifacts, and treasures do they contain?

The Scythians were master horsemen and invented the earliest form of saddle.

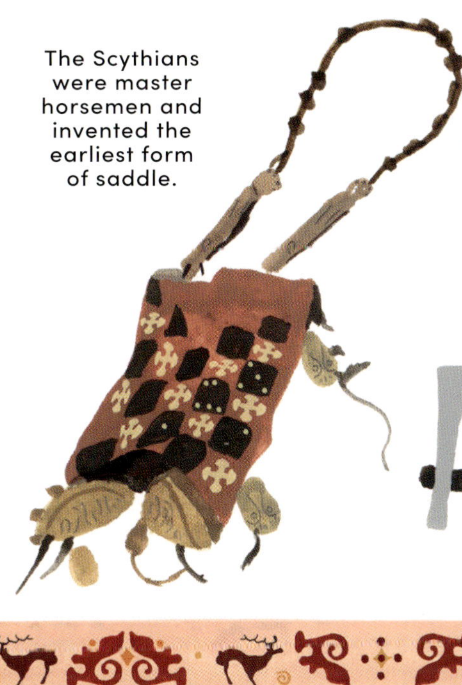

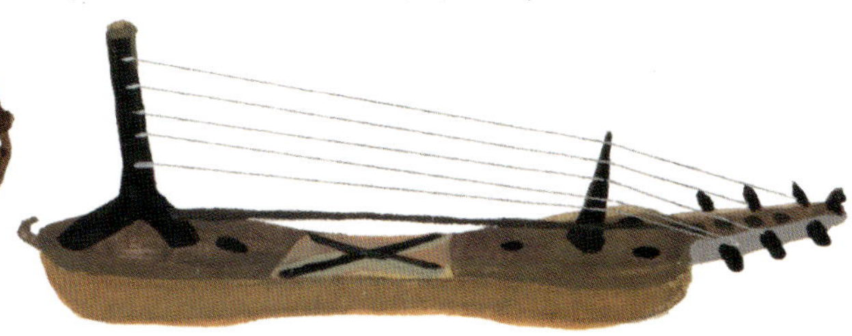

Musical instruments, including horse bells, ancient bone pipes, and a harp have been discovered in Scythian tombs.

The Scythians were fearsome warriors, using swords, pointed battleaxes, daggers, and bow and arrows in battle.

The Ice Maiden

While excavating a kurgan high in the Altai mountains, archaeologists found a single larch wood coffin so long they thought it contained two bodies. Inside was a woman around 25 years old, with tattoos on her arms, lying on her side, facing east toward the rising sun. Scythian women were rarely buried alone, so the archaeologists knew they'd discovered someone important. Whoever she was—perhaps a religious leader or respected storyteller—she died sometime during the fifth century BC.

Tests revealed that this young woman was suffering from cancer. Already weakened by the disease, she suffered a serious fall, perhaps from a horse, shortly before her death. Bedridden but not alone, she was looked after by her people until the end.

The cold preserved the Ice Maiden's clothes: a yellow blouse made from silk that might have come from India, a crimson and white wool skirt, and thigh-high felt leggings. Most spectacular of all was her three-foot-high headdress made from felt-covered wood and decorated with carved birds encased in gold foil. Fashioned to represent the Scythian tree of life, this headdress was the reason her coffin had to be so long.

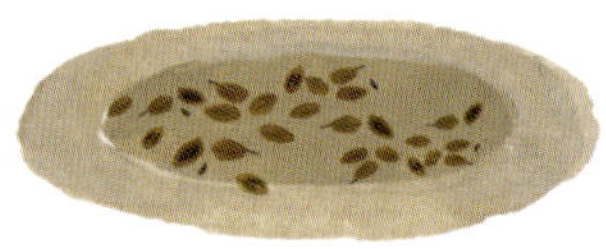

Coriander seeds were placed inside the tomb to scent the air.

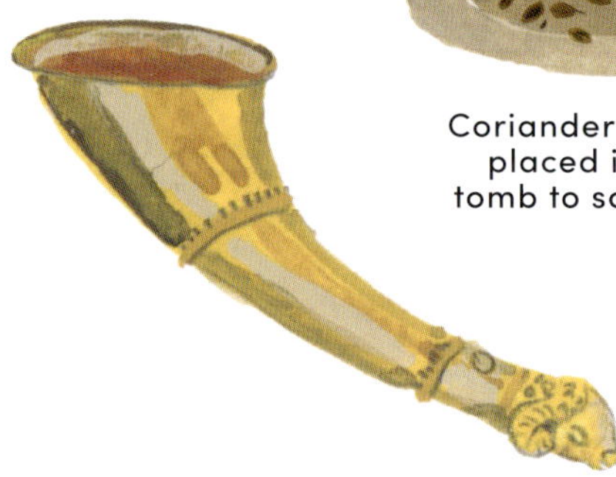

Wealthy or important Scythians drank from animal horns like the yak horn discovered with the Ice Maiden.

The portable table in the Ice Maiden's kurgan had horsemeat and mutton placed on it.

The Ice Maiden's personal belongings included an animal-horn cup, a portable table with removable legs, and a dish containing burnt coriander seeds. Outside the "cabin" were several horses. Their flesh was so well-preserved it gave off a strong smell during excavation. Each had been killed by an axe blow to the forehead—sacrificed so they could escort their mysterious mistress into the afterlife.

Skin-deep Art

Most Scythians were heavily tattooed, and by using black ink made from soot they transformed their bodies into living works of art. Their shoulders, arms, backs, chests, and legs became pastures for grazing herds, hunting grounds for predators, and battlefields for fantastical winged monsters. When a Scythian moved, these beasts moved too—flexing their limbs, arching their backs . . . coming alive.

We don't know why Scythian men and women inked themselves, but it wasn't only because they thought it looked good. It's possible they believed their tattoos gave them magical protection, were used to depict stories from their mythology, commemorated acts of bravery in battle or during a hunt, or were a means of personal identification that even carried over into the afterlife. All we know for sure is that their tattoos and the animals they depict were immensely important.

Of all the tattoos discovered on ancient mummies, those of the Scythians are the most detailed, complicated, and beautiful. The fantastical beasts decorating the Ice Maiden—a deer with ornate antlers, a curly horned ram, and a spotted predator—are full of life and movement, just like the Scythians were themselves.

The Painted Chieftain

A Scythian mummy with particularly spectacular tattoos was discovered in the 1950s. This thick-set, powerfully built man is believed to have been a chieftain.

Although partially decayed, enough of his skin survives to show the intricate and stylized animal tattoos covering his body. These include a donkey, a mountain ram, two deer-like creatures with long antlers and hooked beaks, a fantastical beast on his right arm, two griffins on his chest, and a fish, four rams, and a monster on his right leg.

The Self-Mummifying Monks

What is the one thing you must have if you want to make a mummy? Answer: a dead body. And yet in Japanese temples perched on sacred mountains are the preserved remains of holy men who chose to mummify themselves *while still alive*. It is said that the process—called *sokushinbutsu*—was long, tortuous, and almost beyond belief.

The idea for self-mummification began with a Japanese Buddhist monk named Kūkai (774–835 AD). Kūkai and his followers believed they could gain spiritual strength by enduring physical hardship, such as starving themselves or standing under freezing-cold waterfalls.

At the age of 62, Kūkai took this belief as far as possible. He stopped eating and drinking, entered a state of deep thought called "meditation" and allowed himself to die of starvation. Months later, Kūkai's followers were amazed to find his body untouched by decay and looking much the same as he had in life. Kūkai's incredible preservation was seen as proof that his everlasting spirit had achieved great power. Between 1081 and 1903, several hundred monks attempted to follow Kūkai's path to self-mummification. Only around 20 succeeded.

A monk choosing to undergo sokushinbutsu knew he was beginning a process of extreme hardship that was likely to fail. To succeed, he needed mental strength to cope with the severe physical demands; a body stripped of fat, muscle, and as much moisture as possible to make decomposition less likely, and a calm state of mind at the point of death.

For a monk to self-mummify, he had to reduce the parts of his body that were likely to cause decomposition—the muscles, fat, and water. To do this he drastically changed his diet, and for three years (and often much longer) he ate only nuts, roots, tree bark, and pine needles.

This diet—called *mokujikigyō*, which means "the practice of eating material that comes from trees"—worked alongside a routine of meditation and vigorous exercise that eventually turned him into little more than a living skeleton. When there was no more fat and muscle to lose, the monk allowed nothing to pass his lips except a poisonous tea made from tree sap that made him vomit and sweat, reducing his body's water content even more.

With death close, the monk clambered into an underground chamber just big enough to sit cross-legged in. His followers then sealed the chamber, leaving an air hole and a bell for him to ring to let them know he was still alive. Alone, in the silent darkness, the monk meditated and waited for his body to let go of its grip on life.

When the bell stopped ringing, his followers closed the air hole and left, returning 1,000 days later to see if his body had self-mummified. If he'd succeeded in self-mummifying properly (most did not), they took his preserved body to a temple to be worshipped as a true sokushinbutsu, comforted in the belief that his spirit was watching over them.

Secrets Revealed, Secrets Kept

We have traveled far back in time and widely across the world on our journey to understand the dead. We've trekked up mountains and delved into bogs; we've breathed icy Arctic air and hot desert sand; we've explored colossal tombs and simple dirt-dug graves.

The people we've met—the pharaohs, sailors, and salt miners, the horse lords, marquises, and monks, the noblewomen, ice maidens, and fisherfolk—have revealed many things about themselves; not only physical aspects like their height, hair color, what they ate, and what they wore, but also fascinating insights into their beliefs, customs, and cultures.

We learned that the Inca and the Northern Europeans of the Iron Age valued a human life so highly that they offered them up as the ultimate sacrifice to their gods; that the Chinchorro kept their dead close by for years before burying them in the desert; that the Scythians did not let death part them from their beloved horses, and that some ancient Chinese noblewomen enjoyed eating owl.

Although we can never truly "know" the dead (their living personalities, character, and often their names will forever be their secrets), examining their clothes, belongings, and physical remains does provide rare glimpses of the people they once were—the unique human beings who lived hundreds, and sometimes even thousands, of years ago.

The beautiful tattoos on the Scythian Ice Maiden's arms and hands show us the mythical creatures she believed in and probably told stories about; we can imagine her pain as they were inked under her skin, and her pride when they were finished. The extraordinary preservation of Lady Xin Zhui shows us that even though she ate far more and better food than most of the Chinese population, it made her unhealthy and eventually contributed to her death.

The clothes, weapons, equipment, and medicine that Ötzi carried demonstrate how prepared and skilled he was at surviving in the harsh world of the European Copper Age, and when we gaze into the frozen faces of John Torrington, John Hartnell, and William Braine we really can see what they looked like in the 1840s, right down to the color of their eyes. Such glimpses are precious and remind us that these are not only mummies or skeletons, they are the remains of people who once lived.

And yet many things will remain forever unknown: like why Ötzi, Yde Girl, or Gebelein Man were killed; or what a wealthy man was doing inside a Persian salt mine; or what really happened to Captain James Franklin and his crew; or what killed Tutankhamun, the most famous mummy of all.

There are many more bodies that remain to be uncovered—buried in sand, frozen in ice, or hidden in caves. I wonder who they were, and what new secrets they'll one day share with us?

Where They Were Found

Tollund Man
Denmark
Yde Girl
The Netherlands
The Salt Men of Iran
Iran
Ramses II
Egypt
Gebelein Man
Egypt
Tutankhamun
Egypt
Painted People of the Steppe
Russia
Beauty of Xiaohe
China
The Wet Mummy
China
The Self-mummifying Monks
Japan
Lady Xin Zhui
China

Glossary

AFTERLIFE: The place where some people believe they will go after they die.

ALPACA: A mammal similar to the llama, native to South America.

ANCESTORS: People from the distant past to whom we are related.

ARCHAEOLOGIST: Someone who studies human history by excavating sites and analyzing what they find.

ARTERIES: Large vessels that deliver blood around the body.

BURIAL MOUND: A mound of earth or stones piled over a grave or graves; sometimes called a "barrow" or "tumulus."

CEMETERIES: Areas used for the burial of the dead, like a graveyard.

CIVILIZATION: A complex human society that builds, trades, and creates its own art, culture, and identity.

COCA: A South American plant that was used by the Inca as a powerful drug.

CONQUER: The act of taking over a country, region, or group of people by hostile enemy forces.

CORPSE: A dead human body.

CT SCAN: A "computerized tomography" scan that uses X-rays and computers to create 3D images of the insides of bodies without damaging them.

DECAY: The process by which the soft parts of the body break down and rot away after death.

DECEASED: Another word for dead.

DEMON: A supernatural creature of great power.

EMPIRE: A group of countries or states ruled over by a single person or state.

EXCAVATE: To dig up or expose something or someone, such as a tomb or a mummy.

FERMENTED: A natural process that turns the sugar in fruits or grains into alcohol.

FORENSIC: Modern scientific methods used to investigate crimes or scenes of death.

FUNERAL: A religious ceremony involving the preparation, burial, laying to rest, or respectful disposal of a dead body.

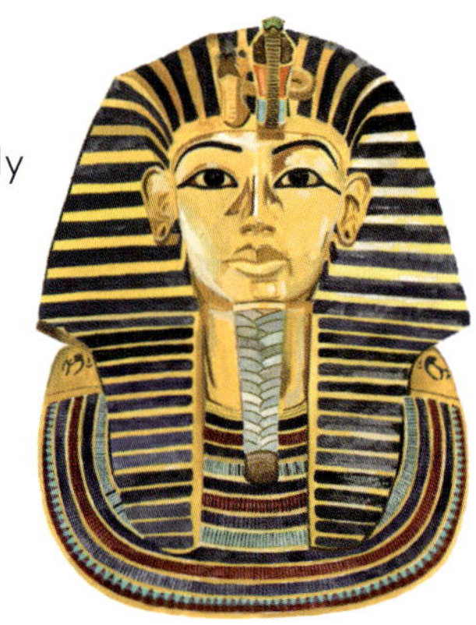

FUNERARY MASK: A mask placed over the face of a preserved body; often highly decorated and made from precious materials.

INCENSE: A material that is burned to produce a pleasant smell.

INDIGENOUS: The first known people in a geographic area, and their descendants.

INTERNAL ORGANS: The internal parts of the body that perform essential functions, such as the liver, kidneys, heart, and brain.

LINEN: A soft material woven from the flax plant.

MAIZE: A plant from Central America, also called "corn" or "sweetcorn."

METEORITE: A piece of metal or rock that has fallen to Earth from space.

MILLENNIUM: A period of time: 1,000 years.

MONASTERY: The buildings and grounds used as a home and place of worship and work by monks.

MUMMY: The naturally or artificially preserved body of a human or an animal.

MYTHOLOGY: A culture or group of people's collected stories and myths.

OFFERINGS: Objects such as food items, animal sacrifices, or figurines left as gifts to the dead, gods or goddesses at tombs, temples, shrines, and by graves.

PARCHMENT: An early form of paper made from animal skins used in ancient and medieval times.

PRESERVATION: The process of keeping something as complete and intact as possible—this can be done deliberately or occur naturally.

QUARRY: A large pit in the ground where stone or other useful materials are dug up.

RADIOCARBON DATING: A scientific method of working out how old an organic object is, such as bones or wood.

REIGN: The length of time that a king, queen, or any royal leader rules their people.

RESIN: A thick, sticky substance produced by trees and plants.

RESURRECTION: The process of a person returning from the dead, believed to exist in some parts of the world and some religions.

REVOLUTIONARY: A brand-new and very different way of doing something.

ROMAN EMPIRE: A mighty empire founded by the Romans, that lasted from 27 BC to 476 AD.

SHABTI: Small statues placed in ancient Egyptian tombs and often shaped like a mummy.

SOFT TISSUES: The parts of the body that connect, support, or surround bones and teeth, including the skin, internal organs, muscles, tendons, ligaments, nerves, fat, and blood vessels.

SOUL: The invisible part of a person that is believed by some people and religions to live on after death.

STEPPE: The vast plains and grasslands of Siberia.

TEXTILE: A type of woven fabric or cloth.

TOMB: A vault, enclosure, structure, or monument for burying the dead that is often underground.

TORSO: The chest, back, and abdomen of the human body.

TREMORS: Vibrations in the ground caused by earthquakes and volcanic eruptions.

VICTORIAN: The period of Queen Victoria's reign: 1837–1901.

WREATH: An assortment of flowers, leaves, and twigs constructed to form a ring. Often placed on graves as a mark of respect.

Index